"I love Christmas stories, and I've writt[...] been writing annual Christmas novels [...] them. This year's novel, *A Husband's Ch[...]* pastor. The story shows just how human the family is. Kathi brings a variety of characters into the story to expand the Christmas theme, at the same time showing growth in the characters of all ages. I highly recommend this wonderful story."

—LENA NELSON DOOLEY, ECPA and CBA best-selling and multi-award winning author of *The Gold Digger*

"Fix your favorite hot drink, curl up in a cozy afghan, and immerse yourself in this delightful read. Within minutes, you'll feel as though you've made a host of new friends whose lives promise to enrich yours. Another winner by Kathi Macias."

—GRACE FOX, author of *Morning Moments with God* and national codirector of International Messengers Canada

"In *A Husband's Christmas Prayer* by Kathi Macias, we meet Diana Michaelson who has everything to be thankful for: a pastor husband, a parsonage, good health, and two wonderful children. So why is she unhappy? Because she mourns the loss of where she used to live—the beautiful house, the church where her husband was the associate pastor, and, most of all, her best friend. Whatever happens in her life simply leaves her discontented as she continually compares the present with the past. Her husband is at a loss as to how to help her. Then Diana meets an older prayer warrior, Virginia, who helps her understand the real meaning of 'home.'"

—DONNA GOODRICH, author of *The Freedom of Letting Go* and *A Step in the Write Direction*

"In *A Husband's Christmas Prayer*, Kathi opens our eyes to God's plans as He molds and uses this family in ways they can't imagine. She beautifully illustrates the temptation to hear God's call on our lives—but, take over and plan how He will work. On the flip side, she also paints a clear picture of the joy in submission to His good plan. This precious story helps us appreciate people we may miss in our own life. A must read."

—LYNDA T. YOUNG, author of the "You Are Not Alone" book series, including *Hope for Families of Children with Cancer* and *Hope for Families of Children on the Autistic Spectrum*

"It's not quite Christmas without a Kathi Macias holiday tale. This is a sweet, relatable story of a young pastor's wife who learns how to faithfully love her husband, children, and new community through changes, moves, and all that comes with a family life. Grab a cup of hot cocoa and enjoy this story of forgiveness, transition, and change."

—SUSAN G. MATHIS, coauthor of *Countdown for Couples: Preparing for the Adventure of Marriage* and *The ReMarriage Adventure: Preparing for a Lifetime of Love and Happiness*

"*A Husband's Christmas Prayer* is an inspirational story of how to face discouragement, even when someone is following God closely. I enjoyed this book because it shows real life—especially in a pastor's home. You'll be rooting for Paul and Diana, as I did. Their narrative is a familiar one and shows God's gentle helping hand."

—KATHY COLLARD MILLER, speaker and author of more than 50 books including *Choices of the Heart*, part of the "Daughters of the King" Bible study series

"In *A Husband's Christmas Prayer*, Kathi Macias creates a heartwarming homecoming story featuring a strong woman of God struggling to be true to His calling as she faces the desires of her own heart. The tension between the two drew me in immediately and kept me hooked to the very last page. Kathi Macias treats the oft-unseen challenges that pastors and their families navigate with dignity and delicacy. A must read for every congregant."

—CATHERINE FINGER, author of the "Jo Oliver Thriller" series,
featuring *Shattered by Death*

"Kathi Macias weaves a story of love, sacrifice, and adjustment to give the reader a glimpse into the life of a pastor with all its ups and downs in dealing with his own family as well as the members of his church. With secondary characters who add warmth and wisdom, this is a story that will both satisfy and delight the reader. I came away with new appreciation for the obstacles facing a pastor and his family, especially when a move is made."

—MARTHA ROGERS, author of the "Homeward Journey"
series, including *Christmas at Stoney Creek*

"Moving a family is never easy, even if it is for a good reason. Kathi Macias's *A Husband's Christmas Prayer* deftly captures the conflict of Paul and Diana Michaelson leaving behind one life for another. As the story unfolds, we see, if we are true to Him and one another in prayer and love, God can guide us to where we need to be. The faith of the characters, the insightful voice of the author, and a story that moves at just the right time and in just the right way are wonderful ingredients in a book that will gently warm your heart."

—MAUREEN PRATT, author of *Don't Panic!
How to Keep Going When the Going Gets Tough*

"If you have ever moved even within your neighborhood, you understand the struggles of the transition. What do you keep, sell, or donate? In a move from one city to another, the emotional pain of leaving church family and longtime friends adds to the turmoil.

"Imagine the intensity of that transition if your spouse doesn't want to move. Pastor Paul Michaelson found himself in that undesirable situation when his wife Diana didn't want to leave their beautiful seacoast town to move to a hot, dry desert city.

"Author Kathi Macias does a masterful job of capturing the emotional roller coaster Diana faces as the pastor's wife in a new home, church, and city that pales in comparison to their previous location. Kathi Macias also succeeds in showing the readers the difficulties the husband experiences. He gradually understands his shortcomings of not praying and discussing the decision with his wife before accepting that senior pastorate.

"As the conflict escalates, God is at work in both the Michaelson family and the small church. Readers will find this a book they're reluctant to put down until they've finished reading it.

"I highly recommend this novel for military families, pastors, those in helping professions, such as counselors and social workers, church libraries, hospitals, and readers who would like to pray more effectively for those in ministry. This book makes a wonderful gift for any time of the year. So buy two: one for yourself and one for someone else."

—YVONNE ORTEGA, author of *Moving from Broken to Beautiful*®

AWARD-WINNING AUTHOR

KATHI MACIAS

A HUSBAND'S
CHRISTMAS
PRAYER

Can he rebuild his marriage
while building a church?

— A NOVEL —

NEW HOPE®
PUBLISHERS
Gospel-Centered. Missions-Driven.

BIRMINGHAM, ALABAMA

New Hope® Publishers
PO Box 12065
Birmingham, AL 35202-2065
NewHopePublishers.com
New Hope Publishers is a division of WMU®.

New Hope Publishers serves its authors as they express their views, which may
not express the views of the publisher.

Library of Congress Control Number: 2016946193

ISBN-13: 978-1-62591-508-5

N174107 · 1016 · 2M1

DEDICATION

To all the wonderful people in my family, especially my husband, Al,
and to the One who paid the price that we might find our eternal
home in His love.

Other books by
Kathi Macias

Pastor Paul Michaelson raked his fingers through his thinning brown hair. His frustration wasn't so much with his wife, who couldn't seem to make the transition from their previous home to this one, it was more with himself for not being more considerate and supportive of her feelings. After all, he was a pastor, and weren't the words "considerate" and "supportive" part of his job description?

He sighed, frustrated with himself for allowing the situation to get to him. "Help me, Father," he mumbled. "Forgive my many failures in dealing with all these changes, and help me to be the husband and father my family needs right now. And as for this congregation . . ." He shook his head. Lately he'd made a bit of progress in getting to know the 40 or so attendees at his fledgling church, but he really missed the "faithful four" who originally came from their recent church to help him plant this new one.

They were gone now, back at Dayspring in Port Mason, California, which he knew was as it should be. But it was just so much easier when they were here. How, then, could he criticize Diana for not successfully making the transfer from the church and home she loved to this new setting? Yet wasn't that what they'd prayed for throughout their seven years of marriage — and even before they took their wedding vows? They both agreed they wanted to serve God, whatever that looked like and wherever it took them. Paul was certain there was no exception clause in that agreement about moving from the lovely seacoast town of Port Mason to hot, dry Desert Sands.

He glanced at his watch. Friday afternoon and nearly time to go home. He sighed as he stood to his feet. Dinner called to him.

How many times had he replayed the scene in his mind? Thirty? Fifty? One hundred? Probably more.

Paul locked up the church and then walked around the pathway to the parsonage in back, the vision of Diana's face teasing his memory as he first told her of his new position as senior pastor at a small town less than two hours away. He had come home with his news ready to burst out of him, certain his wife would share his joy. But the more he told her about their imminent move, the more he came to understand that it wasn't joy he saw reflected on Diana's face.

Sitting beside her on the couch that day, her short blond locks framing the face he loved, he had taken a deep breath and waited for her response. It was a long time coming.

At last she smiled — sort of. He knew that look, though. The smile was forced.

"That's . . . wonderful, sweetheart," she said, laying a hand on his arm. "It's what we've always wanted, isn't it?"

Paul nodded, telling himself he should accept her words at face value but knowing her too well to do so. Even now, her blue-green eyes telegraphed a different message, one that both confused and alarmed Paul.

"Exactly," he said, his eyes still locked on hers and watching for a change. "It's what we've wanted and prayed for, and God has answered our prayers."

She nodded, and her eyes softened slightly. "I suppose He has." She paused, and Paul wondered if he was imagining the hint of tears in her eyes. "So . . ." Diana took a deep breath. "How soon will all this happen?"

"Mark and I will be meeting with the board a week from Thursday to discuss details, but Mark said that as long as everyone concerned feels a confirmation from the Lord, they'd like to get moving on it ASAP." He swallowed. "In a few weeks, actually."

Her eyes went wide. "That soon? But . . . it takes time to pack and move, Paul. We don't even know where we'll be living. And what about the children's school?"

He frowned. "Their school? Diana, they go to preschool two mornings a week. That hardly qualifies as a moving hardship." He cupped her chin in his hand, sorry for his tone. "Forgive me. I know their school is important to you — to us. And as for the quick move, Mark assured me that an entire packing-and-moving crew would be available to us almost immediately." He leaned in and planted a soft kiss on her forehead. "And, sweetheart, even though we're launching a new congregation there, the church building has been around for almost 70 years. It's in a well-established neighborhood." He smiled. "And get this. It even has a parsonage. Mark has seen it, and he says that even though it's a bit older, it's roomy. And it has a huge front porch. Isn't that what you've said you always wanted?"

There was no mistaking the tears that popped into her eyes at that point, and he was relatively certain the porch comment hadn't helped his cause one bit.

"Couldn't we . . ." She took a shaky breath. "Couldn't we just stay here and commute for Sunday and midweek services? Desert Sands isn't that far away — just an hour or so, right?"

He could see the hopefulness on her face now, but he forced himself to speak truthfully and firmly. "No, sweetheart, we can't commute." He took both her hands in his. "It's nearer to two hours, Diana. And you know a senior pastor — not to mention the senior pastor's wife — needs to live close by. We'll be on-call for our parishioners nearly 24/7. Hence, the parsonage behind the church."

He watched the hopefulness fade from her face. Then she sighed and dropped her eyes. "You're right, of course. I was just thinking . . ." Paul again took her chin in his hand and lifted it. "I know, babe. I love it here, too. You've done so much wonderful work in the women's ministry at Dayspring, not to mention the great job you've done decorating this place, and I know it's in a good neighborhood where many of our friends live. But . . ." He swallowed. "I suppose it's . . . it's not too late to turn it down if you really want me to . . ."

His voice trailed off as once again he saw hopefulness light up Diana's face. "Really? You'd turn it down?"

Paul frowned. He hadn't expected that reaction. "Well, yes . . . I suppose I still could, although . . ." He swallowed. "Although I've actually already accepted it. Not formally, of course, but I did tell Mark . . ."

She reached out her hand to stop him as her brow drew together in a frown. "You've already accepted it? Already? Then why are we having this discussion as if I still had some input here?"

Paul's heart squeezed. He hadn't meant to hurt Diana, but it simply hadn't occurred to him that she would be anything but excited about this possibility. *Maybe it'll just take time for her to adjust,* he told himself. *As she begins to see how God is putting this all together for us, surely she'll come around. Meanwhile, I need to be more supportive and considerate. Help me, Lord!*

As the scene faded in his memory, the parsonage came into view, and he breathed a silent prayer that all would be well that evening. Would Diana ever feel at home here? He certainly hoped so, but he was beginning to have serious doubts.

Diana heard the sound of her husband's shoes crunching on the gravel driveway as he approached the house. She glanced at her watch. At least another half-hour until the meatloaf would be done and she could shut off the oven.

She wiped away the sweat on her forehead and underneath her eyes. Would summer ever end? It was the middle of October, for Pete's sake.

At least we had air-conditioning at the other house, she thought, glancing up at the kitchen ceiling. *These overhead fans don't do much but push the hot air around.* Her heart convicting her for the traitorous comparison, she shoved it as far from her mind as possible and put on her "welcome home" smile, determined not to let her husband see her frustration and disappointment.

They met at the front door. Paul immediately pulled her in for a quick kiss but not before Diana saw the unease and concern flit through his soft brown eyes. It was something she'd seen a lot of lately, and she knew exactly where it came from. Though she continued to try to convince her husband that she had successfully made the transition from her lovely home and nearly perfect neighborhood in Port Mason to the seemingly ancient parsonage in the older, rundown area of Desert Sands, she knew he didn't buy it. And why should he? It was the biggest lie of her 33 years of life.

She widened her smile as she looked up at him. With the exception of his thinning hair, his easy-going good looks hadn't changed much during their seven years of marriage. The twinkle in his eyes when he smiled still stole her heart.

"How was your day?" she asked as she slid her hand into the crook of his elbow and walked him into what was probably called a parlor when it was first built. Thankfully this particular room was spacious enough, and the large picture window looking out toward the church let in a decent amount of light. Still, it was so obvious that her modern dark leather furniture had originally been chosen for a more up-to-date setting. And, of course, there was no family room in the parsonage, so the furniture she'd used for that purpose in Port Mason had been given away or sold at their garage sale a few months earlier.

Diana swallowed a sigh as they settled beside one another on the couch. As her husband briefly shared some of the highlights of his day, she listened attentively, wishing she didn't feel so selfish, as she wished that she could also be enthusiastic about the events of her day. Again her heart convicted her, and she struggled to swallow the words she wanted so desperately to say, words that might make her feel better for a while but could also widen the rift between them. And besides, she knew full well that Paul had bent over backward trying to help her and the children make the transition. So why was it still so hard to dismiss the resentment that continued to nag at her daily?

As Paul wound up his report on his day at work, four-year-old Elizabeth Ann — Lizzie to all who knew and loved her — and three-year-old Micah came bounding into the room.

"Daddy's home!" they cried simultaneously as they launched themselves into his arms.

She watched as Lizzie regaled her father with a report of her day, including helping Mommy make cookies and playing outside with her "little brother."

Micah, never pleased when she emphasized "little," piped up immediately. "We had a race, and I won!"

Lizzie, her long brown hair in a ponytail, rolled her eyes. "You won once, Micah. Once!" She smiled smugly and turned back to her father. "I won all the other times."

Diana could nearly see the air go out of Micah's excitement. She watched his shoulders and chin droop. Even his blond curls, slightly longer than she knew Paul would prefer them to be, seemed to sag.

She reached out to brush the locks from his forehead, smiling at the sweat that held them in place. Obviously she wasn't the only one feeling the unseasonable heat.

Unseasonable in most places, she reminded herself. But not in Port Mason. How she missed the ocean breezes that kept the temperature at moderate levels year-round. She could only wonder who in their right mind had picked such a dismal place to start a town, though she had to admit that Desert Sands was an appropriate name.

She took in her entire family with one glance. "How about some apple juice? We can sit outside on the porch and drink it while we wait for dinner to finish cooking." *And then I can finally turn off that oven, and maybe it'll cool off enough for us all to get some sleep tonight.*

Lizzie and Micah quickly expressed their approval, jumping from their father's lap and then each taking a hand in an effort to pull him from the couch. It was a game they'd perfected in the last few months, and Paul readily played along.

"I'm so tired after working all day," he lamented. "I don't think I have the strength to get up off this couch. What am I going to do?"

"You're going to let us pull you up, Daddy," Lizzie declared.

"Get up, Daddy," Micah agreed, pulling even harder on his father's hand.

Paul glanced her way and gave her the playful wink that had always won her over before.

Before. Before we left our beautiful home behind and came here. Tears pricked her eyes at the selfish thought. She knew she had no right to her self-imposed pity party, but she just couldn't seem to escape it. *Sorry, Lord,* she prayed silently. *When am I going to grow up and start acting like an adult? Help me, please . . .*

She smiled in Paul's direction, knowing he was watching her every response and knowing that he wasn't that easily fooled. But it was the best she could do.

Her family made their way to the front door, the children giggling at their father who continued his mock protestations that he was just too tired to take another step.

"Pull harder," Lizzie ordered.

"I am!" Micah insisted.

When she heard the old screen door slam behind them, she sighed and went to the kitchen to pour apple juice into four plastic tumblers. She was determined to see that her family enjoyed their time together, but she worried that she seldom shared their joy anymore.

Paul awoke, sensing that something wasn't right. He reached to Diana's side of the bed and realized she wasn't there . . . again. This night prowling of hers concerned him.

He rose from the bed, barely awake — just avoiding a collision with their chest of drawers as his eyes adjusted to the darkness. Through the years both he and Diana had risen from bed on many occasions and gone to another room to pray and read the Bible. This was different. And it was time they talked about it.

He found her in the kitchen, drinking a cup of coffee and staring into space. Her tear-streaked face and puffy eyes confirmed his suspicions.

He spoke softly as he approached and sat down beside her. "Everything OK, sweetheart? I woke up and you were gone."

Slowly she focused her eyes on his. She nodded. "I'm fine. Everything is fine."

Paul lifted his eyebrows and reached out to take her hand. "Are you sure? It looks like you've been crying."

She dropped her eyes and sighed. "I miss our house . . . and our friends."

"I know. I do, too . . . sometimes." He paused. "But this is our house now, Diana. You know that."

Tears filled her eyes and threatened to spill over onto her cheeks. "I know. And I know I should be grateful. I'm trying, Paul, but . . ."

Her voice trailed off, and Paul told himself he should be encouraged. At least she seemed willing to talk about it. The last couple of times he'd wakened to find her gone, she'd reassured him she was fine and then returned to bed, the conversation closed.

With his free hand he smoothed a stray lock of hair from her forehead, wondering as he often did how someone as beautiful as Diana had even noticed someone like him. A picture of Micah popped into his head, and he smiled at the similarity of the boy's looks to Diana's.

"I know, baby," he said. "I know this has been hard on you."

She shook her head, as if shaking off his touch. But she didn't remove her hand from his. "It shouldn't be. I've always told God I'd go wherever He wanted me to go and do whatever He wanted me to do." She sighed. "I'm also a pastor's wife. I've known from the beginning what was expected of me. And it all seemed so simple in Port Mason." She shook her head again. "What's wrong with me, Paul? I always thought my faith was strong, that my love for you and the children, and of course for God, was enough. What else could I possibly need?"

A stray tear made its way down her cheek, and Paul resisted the urge to wipe it away. "It's not like I don't know how blessed I am," she continued. "So many of our brothers and sisters around the world are suffering for their faith . . . right now, tonight, at this very hour. And here I am, feeling sorry for myself when I have everything any woman could ever want." She lifted her chin and looked directly into his eyes. "Why am I so selfish and immature, Paul? I don't want to be this way — at least, I don't think I do. And I know God wants to change my heart, and most of the time I want Him to. But other times . . ."

She sighed, and her shoulders drooped. "Sure, I miss our house and neighborhood in Port Mason, not to mention our friends and everyone at Dayspring." She shook her head, as if she couldn't quite believe the words she spoke. "I even miss those silly goldfish we left behind with the Kelloggs. I know it made more sense to leave them than to try to bring them with us, but . . . I actually miss the familiar tasks of feeding them and changing the water." She sighed again. "I know. I'm being ridiculous. I never thought I'd be such a baby about moving to a new place."

Paul scooted his chair closer and pulled her into his arms. "You're not being ridiculous," he whispered, stroking her hair.

As she finally relaxed and let the tears fall, dampening the front of his pajama top, he felt his own tears stinging his eyes. *Help me, Father,* he prayed silently. *Show me what to do, what to say . . .*

Then slowly, softly, he began to speak words of encouragement and comfort to his wife — words from Psalm 91, which he knew Diana loved.

"He who dwells in the secret place of the Most High shall abide under the shadow of the Almighty. I will say of the LORD, '*He is* my refuge and my fortress; my God, in Him I will trust.'"

CHAPTER 2

Mitchell Green awoke to a familiar whisper. He knew it could come from only one source.

"I'm awake, Lord," he said aloud. "Do You want me to get up and pray?"

The silent but resounding *yes* was all the answer he needed. At 89, he had walked with the Lord long enough — 75 years, to be exact — to know when he was being called to prayer. And though he'd made it a practice to pray often throughout his lifetime, the call had come more clearly since his beloved Sandra had died a few years earlier.

He slid his feet into his slippers, grabbed his robe, and headed for the spare bedroom, which he'd long since referred to as his "prayer closet."

His Bible lay waiting for him beside the rocking chair. He sat down and opened it to the Book of Psalms — his usual starting place if he had no clear direction otherwise — and began to read aloud from Psalm 139.

"O LORD, You have searched me and known *me*. You know my sitting down and my rising up; You understand my thought afar off. You comprehend my path and my lying down, and are acquainted with all my ways. For *there is* not a word on my tongue, *but* behold, O Lord, You know it altogether."

He set the book down on his lap and closed his eyes. "Psalm 139. One of my favorite passages, Lord, as You well know. But is there something new I need to see here, Father? Something I haven't noticed before?"

He waited, and when no answer came, he decided it wasn't necessary for him to know the details, since God already did. He would pray until God released him to go back to bed. And so, going back and forth from reading a line or two and then praying for peace and mercy to anyone who might need it that night, he continued on until he drifted off to sleep more than an hour later, his head resting against the back of the chair.

Diana slept in later than usual on Saturday morning. She told herself it was perfectly normal to do so after being up for several hours during the night. And besides, no one had to get up early today. Even Paul took it easy on Saturdays, having already outlined his sermon the day before, though she knew he'd carve out some time to go over it and to pray before turning in that night.

She turned her eyes toward her husband's side of the bed, knowing even before she did that he wasn't there. The bed just didn't feel the same without him. And isn't that what he'd told her as he held her last night? He said he'd "felt" her absence and came looking for her.

Tears pricked her eyes as she thought of her husband's tender care and attention as he'd prayed for her only hours earlier. How blessed she was to have such a godly husband — not to mention two adorable and healthy children. So why couldn't she extend her gratitude to take in their new home and church congregation?

She frowned as a faint memory danced through her mind. It had been happening a lot lately, but she always shoved the image away before it took shape. Today was no exception.

Before she could heap more condemnation on herself for her selfish feelings, she threw back the covers and got up, sliding her feet into her slippers in the process. Though they were well into October, she could already feel the old house heating up. In all fairness, their home in Port Mason hadn't been close enough to the ocean to hear the waves, but that had been readily remedied by a 20-minute walk westward.

She stepped from their room into the hallway. Another unwelcome comparison lifted its ugly head. *At least in our other house Paul and I had our own bathroom directly off our bedroom. And there was a full second bathroom in the hallway for the children and guests. Here I have to leave my room to get to the only full bathroom, in the hallway — and hope no one is there ahead of me. I suppose I should be thankful that the last tenants had the good sense to add a half bath off the kitchen . . .*

Enough, Diana. Stop already! No more whining.

She breathed a sigh of relief when she saw the bathroom was open. That either meant the children were still asleep or they were in the kitchen or out in the yard with Paul.

By the time she was out of the shower and had applied a dab of makeup and combed out her damp curls, Diana was feeling a bit more optimistic about the day. *Maybe we can all do something as a family for a change.* Paul had recently confessed to her that his role as senior pastor, even to such a small congregation, consumed more time than he'd bargained for, and he felt badly about not spending more time with her and the children.

As she headed down the hall toward the kitchen, the phone rang. She stopped at the kitchen door and took in the scene. Her children sat, still pajama-clad, at the table eating French toast and bacon, while Paul held the phone to his ear, a deepening frown on his forehead.

Diana knew that look. He wasn't angry; he was concerned. Something was wrong, and she knew without asking that it meant he'd be leaving as soon as he ended the call.

"Good morning, sweetheart," Paul said as he hung up the phone and walked toward her. "I'm so sorry, but I've got to go out. Virginia

Lopez is in the hospital again, and her son wants me to go and pray with her."

She nodded as he pulled her close for a quick kiss.

"As you can see, the kids are fed — though I'd hoped to surprise you and have them dressed by the time you got up. But I shouldn't be long. When I get home, we'll all go do something fun, all right?"

Delighted squeals from Lizzie and Micah interrupted them before Diana could respond.

"Can we go to the park, Daddy?" Micah asked, jumping down from his chair and rushing to wrap his arms around Paul's leg.

Lizzie was right behind, laying claim to his other leg. "A picnic!" she declared. "Let's go to the park and have a picnic!"

Paul chuckled as he broke away from Diana and looked down at their children's expectant, upturned faces. "We'll see," he said, patting each one on the head. "It depends what time I get back . . . *and* how hot it is outside today."

"It won't be too hot," Micah said. "We can wear shorts and bring a fan."

Lizzie rolled her eyes. "We can't bring a fan to the park. Where would we plug it in?"

Micah's eyes narrowed and his jaw twitched before he answered. "We can bring a paper fan like we made at children's church."

"That won't work either, Micah. There's four of us. How's one paper fan going to help?"

Before Micah could carry the argument any further, Diana intervened. "All right. That's enough about parks and picnics and fans for now. Daddy has to go to the hospital to see Mrs. Lopez. And you two need to get back to the table and finish your breakfast."

"What about you, Mommy?" Lizzie asked. "Are you going to have breakfast with us?"

She smiled and nodded. "Just coffee for now. But yes, of course, I'll sit with you while you eat."

As Paul planted a parting kiss on her cheek and headed for the entryway where he kept the keys to his five-year-old gray Toyota Corolla and a small Bible for just such occasions, Diana went to the counter and poured a cup of coffee from the almost-full pot. Food would have to wait until later. For now she'd focus on being grateful for a thoughtful husband who loved God and His people above all else. What more could she ask for?

Paul covered the already familiar drive to the hospital in well under 15 minutes. He couldn't deny how well situated he was in the parsonage — directly behind the sanctuary and his office, and within short commutes to the hospital, schools, and most of his church members' homes.

He parked in a vacant clergy space in the hospital parking lot and headed for the front entrance. In the six months they'd been in Desert Sands, he'd logged in quite a few hospital visits and already felt familiar with the old building.

The woman sitting at the information booth didn't look like anyone he'd seen there before. Apparently he was right because as soon as he told her why he was there, she asked to see his clergy badge then reminded him to keep it on while in the building.

Paul nodded and clipped the badge to his lapel as the volunteer looked up Mrs. Lopez's room number. After getting the number and thanking her, he headed for the elevators.

Once on the third floor, he made his way down the hallway then knocked lightly on the half-closed door. When no one replied, he peeked inside.

The first bed was empty, but the second one, nearer the window, contained a somewhat frail old woman with her eyes closed. He decided not to wake her but to pray for her and then leave. Besides, he knew this dear lady well enough by now to realize she had a strong prayer life of her own, one that no doubt outshone his own many times over.

As quietly as possible, he picked up the metal folding chair by the window and moved it closer to Mrs. Lopez's bed. Then he sat down and silently laid his hand on her arm, marveling at how tissue-thin her skin felt.

Father God, he began silently. Before he could pray another word, the patient's soft voice penetrated his thoughts.

"Pray out loud," she said. "Please."

He opened his eyes and checked her face. Her eyes were still closed, but a faint smile tilted the ends of her mouth upward. He returned the smile then bent his head.

"Thank You, Lord, for this godly woman's life. We know it is Your presence within her that has guided and encouraged her and blessed so many others through her for so many years. Because of Your faithful work within her, when we look at her now, we see You." He took a deep breath and continued. "We ask now that You would touch her as the Healer, and restore her health and strength that she might continue to serve You as she has done for so many years."

Mrs. Lopez's words interrupted him again, this time in a soft but firm request of her own. "And Father God, You know how much I long to come home, to be with You and with so many others who have gone on before me. You are the One who numbers our days, Lord, and only You know how much longer I am to be here in Your service. I ask for the strength to be what You've called me to be for as long as I remain. And when that time is done, Father, I will gladly slip from this earthly body and rejoice in Your eternal presence."

Paul felt humbled. He knew only a little of this woman's history, including the death of her husband and two of their three children. He imagined there had been much more pain and suffering in her lifetime, but she didn't dwell on it. Instead, as she'd told him more than once, she focused on "finishing well."

"Amen," he said, lifting his head to meet her now open brown eyes. Her smile was as gentle as her words.

"Thank you, Pastor. I knew you'd come, though I didn't want to bother you on a day I know you usually reserve for your family. Besides, there's nothing wrong with me. My son worries too much." She smiled and winked, the twinkle in her eye making her look years younger than Paul imagined she really was. "I'll be home by Monday at the latest, you mark my words."

Paul nodded. "Good. I certainly hope that's true. And as for my family and Saturdays, you're right. I do usually spend the day with them, except to break away to go over my sermon for the next day. But even the children are beginning to understand about my calling. A pastor is never really 'off,' I'm afraid."

Mrs. Lopez's smile faded. "Oh, but you need to be," she insisted. "I know you consider yourself on-call 24 hours a day, seven days a week — " she chuckled " — and even that isn't enough for some in the congregation."

The sparkle in her eyes warmed Paul's heart. He had no doubt she meant what she said. "You're right, of course. And I really need to get to that place where I can draw those healthy boundaries and stick to them. But . . ." He paused, his heart suddenly heavy. "Do you think there really is such a place, Mrs. Lopez?"

"Virginia, please," she corrected. "And yes, I do. But you have to seek it diligently and then protect it ferociously." Her eyes narrowed. "I've seen too many pastors' families get shipwrecked for lack of keeping those guidelines."

He nodded again, marveling at the woman's wisdom, even as he dismissed the idea that his family could ever be one of those pastors' families that shipwrecked due to too much stress and too many demands. He grinned. "I think you've been following me."

She chuckled. "Perhaps. In prayer, at least. You do know that I pray for you and your family regularly, don't you?"

"I suspected as much," he conceded. "And it means a lot. It's been tough moving my family from their home. Don't get me wrong. We're thrilled that God has called us to plant and pastor this church, but I won't say it's easy."

"I'd be concerned if you told me it was. Families have a way of putting down roots, and that's as it should be. Just pray and watch carefully about where those roots are actually planted."

Paul blinked, sensing her words were coming straight at him from the Father's heart. "Thank you," he said, scarcely above a whisper. "I needed to hear that."

"I know." She patted his hand. "God is good."

"All the time."

She smiled. "And now will you read a couple of chapters to me? It's difficult for me to hold my Bible while I'm lying down."

Paul made a mental note to bring his ancient tape player and the Bible on tape, both of which were stuffed away somewhere in his office desk. Then he opened the small Bible he'd brought with him and began to read aloud.

CHAPTER 3

By the time she heard Paul's car coming down the gravel driveway, Diana had the children dressed and working on some arts and crafts at the kitchen table. It wasn't the same as the two mornings a week that she'd had them in preschool back in Port Mason, particularly since she no longer had the free time she'd had then, but Lizzie and Micah seemed to enjoy it. Lizzie was especially good at patiently coloring within the lines or cutting out simple designs with her childproof scissors. Micah, on the other hand, could sit still only so long, regardless of how interesting the project might be. It was obvious he was quickly getting to that point right now.

"All right, you two, time to start cleaning up. Daddy's home, and we still have plenty of time for all of us to do something fun together."

She heard the car door slam as Micah looked up, his blue eyes dancing. "Daddy's home? Yay!" He dropped his crayons on the table, hopped down from his chair, and made a beeline for the front door.

Diana sighed. So much for cleaning up first. She knew she should call him back and remind him not to run in the house, but it was obvious from the squeals and laughter coming from the front porch that father and son had already connected.

She laid her hand on Lizzie's head, smiling at the look of concentration on the child's face. "Lizzie, don't you want to clean up and go see Daddy, too?"

"Not yet. I have to finish this first."

"Can't you finish it later?"

"No. It's for Daddy. I want to give it to him now." She finished coloring a section of her page then looked up, smiling.

Diana marveled again at how much she resembled Paul.

"There," the girl announced. "I'm done. Do you think Daddy will like it?"

"He'll love it," Diana confirmed. "And just in time. Here they are!"

Mother and daughter turned toward the kitchen door just as Paul came in with Micah riding on his shoulders.

"I'm a cowboy, and Daddy's my horse," Micah announced as they crossed the room toward the girls.

"So I see," Diana said, lifting her head to return Paul's kiss. She stepped back and nodded toward her daughter. "Lizzie made you something very special."

Paul lifted his eyebrows and turned his gaze toward his daughter. "And what is this very special thing you've made for me, young lady?"

Lizzie's excited expression was muted by apprehension. Diana knew her so well, including how she felt at that exact moment.

"It's our family," she explained, holding up the page she'd been coloring. "Mommy showed me how to draw people with sticks, so I drew you and me and Mommy and Micah. Then I colored us. See?"

Holding Micah's leg with one hand, he reached out with the other to take the colorful paper. He held it close and studied it. "This is amazing, Lizzie. It really does look like all of us. Great job!"

The girl's tentative smile expanded to take in her entire face. "Really, Daddy?"

"That doesn't look like us," Micah said, peering over the top of his father's head. "It looks like stick people."

"Oh, I can definitely tell who's who in this picture," Paul said. "Especially since Lizzie colored our hair and eyes. See, Micah? You have blond hair and blue eyes like Mommy, and Lizzie and I have brown hair and brown eyes." He glanced at the refrigerator. "Well, would you look at that! There's a nice empty spot on the side of the refrigerator. Why don't we put the picture up there so we can all see it?"

Before he could take the picture and move toward the refrigerator, Lizzie took it back from him. "I want to write our names underneath. I was going to do that first, but I ran out of time."

"I think that's a wonderful idea, sweetheart. As soon as you're done, we'll post it. Okay, punkin?"

The girl nodded, already busy writing out their names under their respective pictures. She was just learning to write all of her letters at her preschool in Port Mason, and she loved the practice. Diana looked from Lizzie to Paul, and their eyes met. His smile was warm, and she felt the tug at her heart, reminding her how blessed she was to have such a loving family.

Mitchell Green adored Saturdays. Years earlier, he had looked forward to them as a time of rest from work, a day he could sleep in and spend quality time with his family. But now, with the children and most of the grandchildren long since grown and busy with lives of their own, and with Sandra gone on to her heavenly reward, that reason was no longer relevant. Now he loved Saturdays for one reason: the next day was Sunday.

He smiled as he set up the ironing board so he could press his clothes for the following day. Mitchell had always worn his "Sunday best" to church. He plugged in the iron and blinked back tears as he remembered the many times he'd watched Sandra get ready for church, starting the day before as he did now.

"You all need to pick out your clothes for tomorrow," she'd said to him and to their three children. "You need to know they're clean and ironed and ready to put on in the morning. I don't want anyone running around at the last minute, trying to find something decent to wear." Then she'd zero in on her brood with an expression that brooked no rebellion. "Remember, we are privileged to get to go to church and worship openly. Many Christians around the world can't do that. It's up to us to show God how much we appreciate His many blessings, and one of the ways to do that is to take a little extra time to look as nice as possible before going to the Lord's house. It's the same reason we are *never* late to church. You wouldn't be late to school, would you?"

When the three children confirmed that they wouldn't, she'd add, "So don't you think we should make an even greater attempt to show up at church on time? It's a matter of respect. To come in late is like telling God He's not a priority." She'd lean in a bit closer to her audience and ask, "I know you wouldn't want to do that, now would you?"

This time the response usually came in the form of widened eyes and a slow shake of their heads. By that time, even Mitchell would find himself at a loss for words, knowing Sandra spoke the truth.

"Good," she'd say then, a warm smile replacing her serious expression. "Now let's get going. When we're all through, I have a surprise for you."

Though her words varied a bit from week to week, she never missed the chance to remind her family of the need to honor the Lord and His house of worship. And then, true to her promise, when everyone had accomplished their task of preparing for the next morning, she would unveil their surprise — usually a special snack or treat that she'd declare was "made with love." It was a Saturday tradition that he missed, along with the many other traditions and memories he had shared with his wife over 53 years.

He cleared his throat, refusing to give in to the tears that still threatened. With each passing day, though, he reminded himself that he was 24 hours closer to seeing Sandra again. And, second only to the assurance that he was also 24 hours closer to seeing Jesus face-to-face, that was a promise he held near to his heart, taking great comfort in its imminent fulfillment.

He laid his freshly washed shirt on the ironing board, ready to carry on the tradition his wife had so faithfully modeled to him and their children. As he ironed, he thought of the reason he continued to look forward to Sunday, even though he had to prepare by himself.

They're my family, he reminded himself. *People who love God like I do. People I will spend eternity with. People who stand beside me, not only on Sunday morning when we worship together but also throughout the week.* Mitchell smiled at the realization that he knew there were at least a dozen people he could call on at any time, and they would be there for him. *How could I not love them?*

He spritzed starch onto his shirt collar, the way Sandra had taught him, and imagined how pleased she would have been to know that the old church building was once again being used for worship. It was the building where they'd been married, where they'd come with their young family for years, but also the building that had closed its doors when the church board decided it was time to move to a better area of town. Sandra hadn't agreed with that one bit, but as she'd explained to Mitchell and the children, "The church isn't a building; it's the people of God who worship there. So we will move with the congregation to another building."

And they had done so. Still, because they lived only a couple of blocks from the old building, they drove past it often, and nearly every time they did, Mitchell and Sandra had reminisced about some special memory or event they'd participated in there.

"And now we're back," Mitchell said aloud, speaking to his wife as he often did. "You'd be so pleased, my love — even though most of the old crowd isn't there anymore. But a few of us have come back, and new people from the neighborhood are beginning to find their way there, too." He smiled and nodded as if to affirm his words. "Yes, ma'am, you would most certainly be pleased. And you'd like the new pastor, too. He and his wife have two little ones, and they remind me of our family's younger days." He sighed, ignoring the tug at his heart as he pulled the shirt from the ironing board and immediately placed it on a hanger so it wouldn't wrinkle overnight. Then he went back and began the same process on his slacks, determined to spend as much of the day as possible in prayer for the new pastor and his family, and for the slowly growing congregation as well.

Diana opened the refrigerator and pulled out all the ingredients for a fresh garden salad. Dinner would be light that evening, as it often was on Saturdays after a special family time that nearly always centered on food and fun and left little time for hefty dinner preparations. Once Paul had gotten back home from his hospital visit with Mrs. Lopez, they'd packed a picnic lunch and headed for one of only two parks in town. Thankfully they'd found a relatively cool spot under a tree, and the desert weather had been less brutal than usual.

In spite of the sense of heaviness that seemed to follow her everywhere she went these days, she smiled as she remembered their time at the park. Lizzie and Micah ran and played, quite obviously enjoying every minute of their outing. She marveled at children's ability to enjoy the smaller things of life. They didn't need an expensive vacation to Disney World or even to the beach — though the latter was still at the top of their entire family's favorites list. Her children relished everything they did together. How was it possible that she had lost so much of that ability to appreciate the simpler things in life? Then again, it seemed lately that she struggled to enjoy bigger events as well. And deep down, she knew it had to do with the vague, disturbing thoughts and heaviness of spirit that plagued her lately.

It had started when Paul first told her about their impending move. She'd found herself dragging her feet, refusing to jump in and wholeheartedly support her husband, even though she knew it was a move they'd spoken of and prayed about many times over the years. And her refusal — or inability — to rejoice with Paul only served to increase the heaviness.

What kind of wife and mother am I? It wasn't the first time she'd asked herself such a pointed question. And it certainly wasn't the first time she'd concluded that she was lacking on all fronts.

Since Paul and I began dating, all I ever wanted was to build a life with him, have a family, minister together. So what's wrong with me, Lord? Why am I resisting what is obviously Your will and purpose for us?

She sighed deeply, something she caught herself doing far too often these days. But she brushed it away as she began to slice the tomatoes. Was it too warm for soup? Not if they sat outside in the breezeway to eat, she decided. And her family would no doubt love it — one more fun thing to do together before the day came to an end.

And then it's off to church in the morning, she reminded herself. *Oh, Father, will I ever get past missing our Port Mason home and congregation? I know Paul needs me to help build this fledgling congregation, and I'm doing what I can — at least I think I am. But it would be so much easier if my heart was in it . . .*

CHAPTER 4

Paul had headed over to the church while Diana and the children were still eating breakfast. They always joined him just before service began, but if they didn't move a bit quicker, they'd never make it on time.

"Micah, quit playing with your eggs," Diana said. "We're going to be late."

"I told him that, Mama," Lizzie said, her own plate nearly empty, "but he doesn't listen."

"I do, too," Micah argued, lifting his head and glaring at his sister. "And you're not my mom."

Lizzie huffed, her brown eyes widening as she glared back. "I don't have to be Mom, but I can tell you to eat."

"Cannot!" Micah insisted, his cheeks reddening.

Before either of them could utter another word, Diana stepped in. "All right, that's enough, you two. Just finish your breakfast and take your plates to the sink. You need to get dressed."

Lizzie's expression changed immediately as she gazed up at her mother imploringly. "Can I wear my new coat? I really love it."

"I know you do, but no, you can't wear it today. That's for when the weather gets cold. It's still too warm for coats."

Lizzie's shoulders drooped, and the sparkle in her eyes faded. "It's not fair."

"Is too," Micah said, jumping in uninvited. "Mom gets to tell us what to do."

Lizzie shot a silent dart at her little brother, just as Diana raised her voice a notch. "All right, that's it. Lizzie, clear your plate and go get dressed. We picked out your clothes last night, so it shouldn't take long. And Micah, eat three more bites — *now*. Then scoot to your room and get dressed. I laid out your clothes on your bed."

"Does that mean I don't have to put my plate in the sink?" Micah asked, his blue eyes hopeful as they darted to the small child's step stool strategically placed in front of the sink.

Diana frowned. "Of course you do. Why would you ask?"

The little boy shrugged. "You didn't say to put my plate in the sink."

Diana took a deep breath. She dearly loved her children, but there were times . . .

"Eat three bites," she said, holding his gaze. "Then put your plate in the sink and get dressed — in that order. Understood?"

He nodded and scooped a small portion of scrambled eggs — no doubt cold by now — onto his fork.

Diana stood right there and watched him. Experience told her that if she didn't, he'd dawdle so long she'd finally have to excuse him from the table so they wouldn't be late. She hoped the day would improve as it went on.

The children were finally dressed and ready to go, and after a quick peek at her makeup and hair — she'd long since given up on doing anything elaborate with her unruly blonde curls, other than keeping them short — she decided things were as good as they were going to get.

"Time to go," she announced, herding Lizzie and Micah toward the front door. "We don't want to be late. Daddy will be waiting for us."

"I don't want to sit with Daddy in the big church," Micah grumbled. "It takes too long."

"Now, Micah, you know the children always sit with their families for worship. You and Lizzie can go to children's church after that."

"It still takes too long."

"No, it doesn't," Lizzie said as they stepped off the porch and headed for the front of the church. "I like sitting with Mommy and Daddy in the front row. It means we're special."

Diana raised her eyebrows. "Special? You mean because Daddy is the pastor?"

Lizzie nodded, her ponytail bouncing. "Yep. And everybody knows it because we're in the front row and they're not."

As they rounded the walkway toward the main entrance, Diana lowered her voice. "Sweetheart, you *are* special. We all are because we're part of God's family, and He loves us very much."

"I know that, Mommy," Lizzie conceded. "But I think He loves us more because Daddy's the pastor."

They were very near the front door now, so Diana decided to postpone this "teaching moment" until later. "We'll talk about that later," she said as the bells began to chime, calling them to worship.

A sharply dressed elderly man, whose name Diana knew she should remember but couldn't, stood just outside the doorway, greeting people and handing out bulletins as the sun shone on his nearly bald head. Diana couldn't help but remember that it had taken three or four people to do that job at their last church, simply because there were so many more people in the congregation.

Stop comparing, she told herself. *You do that nearly every time you walk in this door, and it's just not right. This is where God has called you—to stand beside your husband and help him build this church.* She smiled what she hoped was a warm and genuine smile and shook hands with the man whose name she still couldn't remember.

"Good morning, Mrs. Michaelson. Beautiful morning, isn't it?" His smile widened. "You and your children look especially nice today."

Lizzie and Micah, wide-eyed, looked up at their mother, as if waiting for a confirmation before they answered. Bits of the morning they'd spent racing around and arguing, as Lizzie begged yet again to wear her new coat and Micah complained about the pants Diana had insisted he wear, flashed through her mind. She blushed at the memory — and the realization that she hadn't once told Lizzie and Micah how nice they looked.

She nodded at her children and thanked the man, whose name continued to escape her. "Thank you," she said. "And yes, it is a beautiful morning." Taking the bulletin from his hand, she hustled the children into the foyer and straight through into the sanctuary.

Lizzie walked a few steps ahead, being the first to arrive and sit down on the front pew next to her father. The expression on the girl's face as she looked back over the rest of the small congregation reminded Diana that she mustn't forget to have that talk with her daughter about what it really meant to be "special."

Mitchell Green had finished handing out bulletins and now sat in the back of the church as the service began. As he joined others in singing praises to the God he truly loved, he couldn't help but notice how empty the church seemed compared to what it had been years earlier when he and Sandra attended here regularly. Still, he was grateful that God had reestablished this church and called him to be part of it. Though he'd grown close to many in the congregation he'd attended these last years, it was good to be back at Desert Sands Community.

A bit like coming home, he thought, a smile teasing his lips as he continued to sing. *I just wish you were here to share this homecoming with me, Sandra.* But even as the thought danced through his mind, he immediately reminded himself that his homecoming to Desert Sands Community didn't begin to compare to the homecoming he would experience when he breathed his last on earth and, in Sandra's words, "graduated to heaven."

He blinked back the hint of tears that stung his eyes and tried to focus on the words of the song displayed on the screen on the wall behind the pulpit. But then his thoughts veered off as he remembered how much Sandra had loved to sing and how people continually remarked on her amazing ability to do so.

For just a moment, the icy fingers of fear tried to wrap themselves around his heart. *I can't remember what her voice sounded like. How can that be? I loved listening to her sing — not just here at church but at home, when she was washing dishes or folding laundry.* The threat of tears returned, but he shook his head to dismiss it.

No, he would not allow anything to steal his joy at being in church, worshiping and praising the one true God — the One who would one day soon take him home, where he would no doubt hear Sandra singing again. The reassurance melted the icy fear that often came to do battle with him and try to rob him of his peace. "Thank You, Lord," he whispered. "Thank You."

As the singing came to a close and the congregation took their seats, Mitchell's eyes caught the grinning face of the pastor's daughter, looking out over the congregation before her mother motioned to her to sit down and look forward. Mitchell grinned in return, remembering the many times Sandra had called their brood to attention and insisted they sit still and pay attention in church.

Ah, how the years fly by! Mitchell sighed as he settled into his seat and opened his Bible. *I wonder if the young pastor and his wife have any idea how quickly this will all be behind them. Oh, Lord, help them see how precious every moment is when we're serving You!*

Tucking away his thoughts about the Michaelsons, he adjusted his glasses so he could better follow along as the pastor read the day's passage. His eyes weren't what they used to be, but his memory was as sharp as ever. If he couldn't quite make out each word on the page, he most likely knew it anyway. He never regretted the habit his own parents had instilled in him as a little boy. "Memorize a verse each day," they'd told him. "Just one; it doesn't have to be long. It will see you through the tough times and keep you humble when rejoicing in the good."

He nodded. Wise words from wise parents. *Thank You, Lord, for allowing me to be raised by such godly people.*

The pastor finished reading the passage and asked everyone to join with him in prayer. Mitchell Green gladly closed his eyes and bowed his head. He had learned through the decades that bowing in prayer was indeed the greatest position for receiving victory.

When Diana opened her eyes and glanced at the clock beside her bed, her first thought was that someone had forgotten to wake the sun. It was nearly 8 o'clock. She had overslept and oddly Paul's alarm hadn't gone off yet. Though he didn't have much of a commute to work, he liked to be in his office by this time of day.

Then she remembered. *It's Monday—Paul's day off.* She sighed and relaxed into her pillow. She hadn't been able to find a preschool that she both liked and could afford, so Lizzie and Micah didn't need to get up and get ready either.

Smiling, she turned her head and looked at her sleeping husband. This was definitely the man she wanted to wake up beside for as long as she lived.

You have so blessed me, Lord, she thought. *I know I don't deserve it, but I do thank You—*

Wait a minute. She frowned, realizing what was missing. Sunlight! Even in October, the sun was up long before this.

She got out of bed, shivering at the cool air that greeted her. She slid her feet into her slippers and grabbed her robe, tying it loosely around her before leaving the room and walking to the front door. When she pulled it open, she blinked at how gray the sky looked. True, they'd experienced some cool weather and even a little rain when they first moved here in April, but that had quickly given way to the day-after-day sameness of sunshine — and heat.

Diana smiled. "Thank You, Lord," she declared aloud. "It's not hot!"

She heard Paul chuckle and turned to find him standing behind her. "Sounds like it's going to be a good day — a cool one. If I'd known a little gray sky would make you this happy, I'd have ordered one weeks ago."

Diana couldn't help but grin. "You mean you didn't? I thought for sure you had something to do with this, that you asked God to give us a break from the heat."

Paul reached out and drew her into his arms, where she rested her head against his pajama-clad chest. For a brief moment, she remembered doing the same with her father when she was no older than Lizzie. Hearing that strong, steady heartbeat had made her feel safe then — and it did the same now.

"The kids aren't up yet," Paul said. "How about sharing a cup of coffee — together and *alone*?"

She smiled and leaned her head back to look up into Paul's dark eyes. He was only a few inches taller than her, but his arms felt so strong around her. "I'd love that," she said.

Virginia Lopez had been home from the hospital for several hours now and was feeling much better. Her son had picked her up at the hospital and then hung around when he got her home, fussing over her until she sent him away, saying she needed some peace and quiet so she could get some sleep. But she'd no sooner lay down on her bed than her eyes popped open.

"Phooey," she'd said aloud. "Probably slept too much at the hospital. Nothing else to do there. I didn't even have a roommate to talk to."

She got up and walked to the kitchen to make some tea. Even though it wasn't actually cold outside, the sky was gray and there was at least a hint of fall in the air.

"Just enough to make my old bones think about something warm." She filled the kettle, put it on the stove, and lit the burner. Then she went to her special "stash" and picked through the offerings. Citrus tea, peppermint tea, and chamomile . . . then she spotted it. No doubt the last of her White Chocolate Obsession tea bags. She felt sure she'd used them all.

"What a nice surprise, Lord." She smiled. "You *are* going to join me, aren't You?" Virginia talked to the Lord a lot these days. It wasn't so much that she had no one else to talk to; she could call her family or one of her friends from church, of course. But she never tired of being in her Savior's presence. Who else could compare with that?

When the tea was ready, she sat down at the little butcher-block table in the corner, directly across from an empty chair. Unlike the other three chairs at the table, she never pushed that one in. She liked to think of it as her special "guest" chair, and more often than not, it was Jesus who sat there to keep her company.

She said a quick prayer of thanks over her tea. As she took the first sip, she felt its delicious warmth permeate her body. It was as if the ice around her bones had begun melting.

"As You know, Lord, sometimes my bones are cold even when the temperature is in triple digits outside." She sighed. "Now that the day is somewhat cooler, it makes me think about cooking something warm." She grinned and sat up straight at the next thought that popped into her mind. "*Albondigas* soup! Oh, Lord, I haven't made that in several years. I wonder if I even remember how."

She could almost picture Jesus' smile as she rose from the table. She opened the cupboard where she kept her favorite cookbooks and began to thumb through them.

"Bingo!" She held up the open book so Jesus could see the picture. When she was sure He had approved, she took the book to the table to read through the ingredients. She was going to need to make a trip to the store, despite the fact that her son kept threatening to take her car keys away.

"You can't see, Mom," Albert would say. "At least not well enough to drive. And let's face it — your reflexes aren't what they used to be."

She'd harrumphed and challenged him at every point, but finally they agreed to a compromise. She would restrict her driving to Desert Sands — and so far she'd kept that promise. Now she decided that the very next time Albert stopped by, she'd convince him to take her to the grocery store, even though her cupboards and fridge were fairly well stocked. But she knew it made him feel needed, and that was something she understood only too well.

As she studied the recipe in more detail, her tea grew cold. But she wasn't concerned, and she knew she wasn't alone. In fact, the company couldn't possibly get any better.

Paul spent a restful Monday at home with his family, something he tried to do whenever possible. But now it was Tuesday, time to get back to work and start figuring out what to do next.

He'd been the pastor of Desert Sands Community Church for slightly over six months now, and though he wasn't foolish enough to think it would return to its one-time size of several hundred members, he had certainly hoped to far surpass the 40 or so who regularly attended. He'd set out with partners from Dayspring to plant the church, or "replant" it. *It's not like a thriving church didn't exist here at one point. And yet the leadership thought it was time to move to a new location.* He frowned. *Help me to better understand the history of this church, Lord. Was the leadership indeed following your leading when they moved? I imagine they were; after all, the congregation continued to grow and prosper in their new location. But why wait so many years before You called someone to reopen a church here? It seems such a waste for this old but excellent facility to sit empty for as long as it did.*

He thought back to the first time he'd been approached by the leadership at his former church, asking if he'd be open to planting a church in an already existing facility. Since he'd long desired to move on and become a senior pastor somewhere, it hadn't occurred to him that it would be so near, scarcely two hours away. But the more he thought and prayed about it, the more certain he became that this was God's leading.

An invisible band tightened around his heart. Why, then, if it was indeed God's leading, had Diana resisted the move?

What is it, Lord? How do I break through that wall she's put up? She's still a wonderful wife and mother, but as far as embracing this new congregation as a pastor's wife should, she simply hasn't done it. Help me, Father. Show me what to do to help her.

The office phone jangled then, demanding his attention. The phone was a carryover from the previous congregation, a touch-tone with blinking lights for the various church lines but no caller ID. He lifted his chin and reached for the receiver. It didn't matter who it was. In fact, it was probably a good idea to keep this phone so he wouldn't start the practice of deciding beforehand whether or not he would answer. If someone needed him and called, he would respond.

CHAPTER 6

Paul walked home for lunch, as he often did. It had been a relatively slow morning, with only a couple of calls, one from a woman in the church who wanted to know when the next church potluck would be. When Paul said he wasn't sure, the woman asked why. "Isn't your wife the head of women's ministries? Surely she knows the importance of potlucks."

The woman hadn't elaborated on what that importance might be, but Paul had promised to look into it and get back to her. Other than that, he'd spent the morning in prayer and Bible reading, then pored over the church finances — such as they were. Though he tried to conserve where he could, the drafty old church was expensive to heat and cool. He wondered if that fact had been at least somewhat responsible for the previous congregation's decision to move to a newer building.

He had also gone over the church's weekly giving and reaffirmed what he already knew: If Dayspring hadn't committed to pay his salary for at least the first year, he and his family would be destitute. But the small congregation simply couldn't generate enough funds to supply even the most basic needs for his family. The bottom line was, they had to bring in new congregants if Desert Sands Community was ever to become self-supporting.

He stepped up on his porch and reached for the front door. *Forgive me, Lord. I know we can't grow or sustain this church; only You can do that. But I can't imagine that You wouldn't want us to somehow participate in that. Please show us, Father.*

When he stepped into the entryway, Lizzie nearly launched herself into his arms, with Micah right behind. Cries of "Daddy!" warmed his heart, reminding him of how truly blessed he was.

"Want to see my project?" Lizzie asked, her brown eyes dancing. "I've been working on it all morning."

"Me too," Micah added. "I made a project, too."

Paul smiled. "And I would love to see them. Where are they?"

"In the kitchen," the children chorused, wriggling to get down before they raced for the kitchen with Paul following close behind.

Diana didn't even look up when he walked in. She was on her knees, wiping up a large multi-colored puddle beside the table.

"Looks like one of our artists spilled something," Paul commented. "Can I help you with that?"

Diana raised her head. Sweat beaded her brow, and her smile appeared strained. "Thanks, but I've nearly got it." She flashed a stern look at the children, whose excitement visibly ebbed as she scolded them. "Elizabeth and Micah have been using watercolor paints today, and they were just about to clean up their mess when they heard you at the door. It was another one of their arguments that resulted in this mess."

Paul thought that some spilled water on an easily cleanable floor wasn't really much of a mess, but he wasn't about to say so. "Well, then, I'd say they're the ones who should be down on the floor mopping up their mess, not you."

He stepped over to Diana and reached down to gently pull her to her feet. "Lizzie, you and Micah come and clean up the mess you made. Your mother has enough to do."

"But . . . we want to show your our projects," Lizzie said, her chin nearly quivering.

"Yeah," Micah added.

Paul swallowed the smile that threatened to pop out at the look on his children's faces. "I'm sorry," he said. "Clean up the mess first, and then we'll look at your artwork."

Lizzie sighed and hung her head, then knelt down next to the puddle and took the rag Diana had been using. Micah glanced around and said, "I don't have a rag."

Paul quickly grabbed a couple of paper towels and handed them to him. "This will work. Now let's get done so we can see your projects and then have some lunch."

Diana's eyes widened at his words. "Lunch! Already? Oh, Paul, I'm so sorry. We got so caught up in all we were doing that I didn't realize the time. I'll make some sandwiches. It won't take but a minute."

Paul laid his hand on her arm. "How about if you and I make lunch together? That way, when Lizzie and Micah are through cleaning up, we'll all be ready to eat."

Diana's smile was tentative. "Sure. Sounds like a plan."

Impulsively he put his arm around her waist and drew her close, planting a kiss on her forehead as she gazed up at him. "I love you," he said, then released her and went to the fridge to pull out the sandwich fixings they needed.

Diana walked up and down each row in the sanctuary, checking to make sure Lizzie or Micah hadn't missed anything. So far it seemed they'd done a surprisingly good job.

It had all started over lunch. The mess on the kitchen floor had been cleaned up, Paul had *oohed* and *aahed* over the art projects, and they'd all sat down to share their sandwiches — turkey and Swiss for everyone except Micah, who was on a peanut butter kick and refused to eat any other type of sandwich.

As Paul filled them in on the day so far, he mentioned that he'd had a call from Rose Landry, letting him know she wasn't feeling well and wouldn't be in that day to do her usual Tuesday cleanup of the sanctuary — something she'd done for years when the former congregation was there and had then picked up where she'd left off when this new congregation had reopened the doors. He'd assured the feisty octogenarian that it was fine, he'd cover it, and then prayed for her to recover quickly.

"So you had to clean the sanctuary yourself?" Diana asked.

"It's not really a hard job," Paul assured her. "Just a quick pick-up of any leftover bulletins or other items that might have been left behind on Sunday morning. But no, I haven't done it yet. I plan to this afternoon."

"I'll do it," Diana had offered, though she'd been looking forward to getting a little rest this afternoon if she could convince the kids to take naps — which didn't happen often anymore, especially with Lizzie. But Diana had realized that cleaning the sanctuary after Sunday service was something the pastor's wife of a small church should do, especially when the volunteer had to cancel.

So now, here she was, following her children up and down the rows, making sure everything was picked up nice and neat. She knew one of the retired men in the church already donated his time on Saturday to vacuum the sanctuary, as well as the other rooms in the building, while his wife dusted and ran off bulletins for Sunday morning. For that reason, she'd never felt the need to offer to help prepare the sanctuary for service, and she hadn't worried about cleaning up afterward either, since Rose Landry seldom missed.

Seldom, but not never, she mused. *I do remember she missed a couple times over the summer when the heat was too much for her. Did Paul cover that duty himself?* Diana imagined so and felt more than a little guilt that she hadn't stepped in to help.

But how would I know if he didn't tell me? I'm not a mind reader.

She caught herself then, not liking the snarky attitude she heard in her silent words. *Forgive me, Lord. I—*

"Can we go see Daddy now?" Lizzie asked, interrupting Diana's thoughts. "We cleaned it up good enough."

Micah threw in his two cents. "Yeah, good enough."

Diana raised her eyebrows. "You think so?"

They nodded, Micah's blond curls scarcely moving, while Lizzie's brown ponytail bobbed from her exuberance.

"Yes," Lizzie said. "Nobody sits in the back rows anyway."

"And how do you know that?" Diana asked.

"Because I always look back at everybody when I'm sitting up front with Daddy. I bet they wish they could sit up front where we are."

Diana leaned down closer to her children, who waited expectantly, their faces aglow. "When we come here on Sunday morning or Wednesday evening, who do we worship?"

Lizzie spoke first. "Jesus."

Micah nodded. "Jesus."

"Exactly." Diana smiled her approval. "And the Bible tells us that whenever we get together with other Christians, Jesus is here with us. Do you believe that?"

This time they both nodded.

"So . . . we want to do our best job for Jesus, don't we? And that includes cleaning the back rows."

One set of brown eyes and one of blue opened wide. "Come on, Micah," Lizzie said. "Let's go do the last rows." Her final comment was emphatic. "But then we're going to Daddy's office."

Diana's smile widened as she watched them go toward the back of the church and begin their row-by-row inspection. Surprisingly their little cleaning jaunt had turned into a teachable moment, and she was pleased.

Paul wrapped up some last-minute details before locking his office and heading home. He smiled at the memory of his two children knocking on his office door a couple hours earlier and bursting into his office when he called, "Come in." To be honest, he'd been enjoying the quiet and had hoped for a bit more before day's end, but he couldn't very well make himself available to his parishioners and not to his own children.

"We cleaned, Daddy," Micah announced, for once getting his comment in ahead of his sister.

Not to be outdone, Lizzie declared, "We even cleaned the back rows, so when Jesus sits there He won't see a mess."

Diana had walked in behind them, stopping just inside the door and smiling as she watched her little ones chatter excitedly to their father. At one point, Paul had looked up and caught his wife's eye. He smiled and tried to convey a silent thanks. Then he'd sent them all off with a hug, a kiss, and a promise to play with them after dinner.

As he made his way from his office, making the rounds of the building to be certain everything was locked up tight, he smiled in anticipation of spending an evening with his family. Though he often went home exhausted and wished for a quiet evening, he never ceased to be stunned at those who made the decision to walk away from their spouse and children to start a new life, usually with someone else. Though he understood sin and its influence on people's decisions, even those who called themselves Christians, it was beyond his wildest imagination to even consider doing something like that to his own family. Next to his relationship to his Lord, the relationship with his family took precedence over everything else.

He finished locking up the church for the night and soon found himself humming "I'd Rather Have Jesus" as he approached home. He'd already grown to love the sprawling front porch and had no problem overlooking some of the older house's shortcomings. *I certainly have enough of my own*, he reminded himself, chuckling before he returned to humming.

Before he could step up onto the porch, Lizzie and Micah nearly flew out the door, calling "Daddy! Daddy!" as each grabbed a leg and gazed up at him, Micah bouncing on his toes with obvious excitement.

"Let's play Candy Land, Daddy," Lizzie said, her sweetest "daddy's girl" smile wrapping his heart around her little finger. "You promised, Daddy. Remember?"

"Yeah, you promised," Micah echoed.

Paul stooped and knelt down so he could take one in each arm and pull them close. "I promised to play with you," he said, "but I didn't say anything about Candy Land. We'll talk about that . . . *after* dinner. Mommy's been busy cooking a nice meal for us, and we need to go see if we can help her. What do you say?"

Micah's shoulders drooped and his lower lip came out. Lizzie, on the other hand, brightened at the suggestion. "I know how to set the table," she declared. "I'll go do it right now."

"I want to help," Micah called, pulling away from Paul to follow his sister into the house.

Chuckling, Paul followed. It promised to be a great evening.

And it was — until the phone rang in the middle of dinner. Paul wished he had the luxury of saying, "Let it go to voice mail; I'll return the call later." But he was the pastor, and he owed it to his congregation — however small — to be available when they needed him.

He'd excused himself from the table and gone out into the hallway, pacing as he often did when on the phone. By the time he returned to the kitchen, his heart was heavy, having promised a church member he'd go with him to the jail to find out about his 17-year-old son who'd just been arrested.

He stepped up to his spot at the table, but he didn't retake his chair. "I have to go," he said, realizing his wife had known what he would say before he said it.

Diana nodded as the children whined their disappointment. "We understand, don't we?" she asked, looking from one child to the other. "It's Daddy's job."

"But you said you'd play with us," Lizzie said, her accusatory brown eyes piercing his heart.

Micah's chin quivered. "You promised."

"I know I did," he said. "But this is something I have to take care of right now. If I get home before bedtime, we'll play then. If not, there's always tomorrow."

"In the meantime," Diana inserted, "we need to pray with Daddy before he leaves." She stood and walked toward Paul, her hands outstretched to the children. "Come and join us for family circle time. Come on now. Daddy needs to leave."

Paul's heart ached, both with disappointment at letting his children down but also with love for his wife who had stepped in and taken hold of the situation. She may have preferred to be living back in Port Mason, but she was a good wife and mother wherever she was.

Help me to make it up to them, he prayed silently, as he listened to his wife pray for him and for the situation, and then to his children joining in.

"Take care of Daddy," Lizzie said, "but please don't let it take too long. We want to play with him before bed. Amen."

"Before bed," Micah echoed. "Amen!"

In moments he was in the car and on his way. Paul wondered how he would feel if he were in this man's shoes. His heart squeezed at the thought. Yes, he was doing what he had to do in leaving his family behind to accompany this man on what was no doubt a very difficult experience.

CHAPTER 7

Diana allowed the children to stay up nearly an hour past their usual bedtime, in hopes Paul would get home in time to at least kiss them goodnight. But his last text to her said he could be another hour or two.

She'd sighed and put Micah in bed, despite his protests, and he'd been asleep by the time she turned out his light. It was a different story with Lizzie.

"I don't want to go to bed yet. I want to wait up for Daddy."

"I know you do, sweetheart," Diana had conceded as she fluffed her daughter's pillow and tucked in the blankets. "But it's late, and Daddy won't be back for a while yet."

Lizzie huffed, crossing her arms as she pouted. "It's not fair. Daddy works too much. When he comes home, he shouldn't leave again until morning."

Diana smiled and smoothed back a bit of Lizzie's hair from her face. She knew what she had to say, and she knew it was absolutely true, but she felt like such a hypocrite saying it. "Honey, you know we've told you before that Daddy has a very special job. He's a pastor, and he has to help care for the people in the church whenever they need him."

Her bottom lip came out a little more. "It's still not fair."

Diana sighed. "You're right. It's not fair. Many things in life aren't fair, sweetheart. But God loves His people — *all* of them — and He chooses certain ones to help take care of them. And that means they have to take care of others whenever those people need it. Do you understand?"

Lizzie shrugged her shoulders, and her pout softened. "Maybe. Does that mean God chose Daddy to take care of the people at church?"

"It does, yes. And other people, too, but especially those at our church."

Her lips drew into a thin line before she spoke. "Well, I wish God would have picked someone else."

Diana blinked back the hot tears that pricked her eyelids. "Sometimes I wish that, too, Lizzie. But deep down I really want your daddy—and all of us—to obey God. If we say we love God, then we need to be willing to do whatever He wants us to do, even when it seems unfair." She cupped her daughter's chin in her hand. "It is a very special thing to serve God, and that's something we all want to do, right?"

The girl nodded, though with an apparent lack of enthusiasm. Then she brightened, and her eyes went wide. "Is that why I feel special when I sit in the front row with Daddy?"

Diana raised her eyebrows. She'd been telling herself she needed to have this talk with Lizzie at some point, and this seemed to be that point.

"In some ways, yes, that *is* why you feel special when you sit up front with Daddy. And that's all right, as long as we remember that the only reason your daddy sits up front like that is because God chose him to be the pastor of this church. It isn't because Daddy is better than anyone else; it's because he said yes to God." With her child's chin still cupped in her hand, she leaned in and kissed her on the forehead. "And that's what makes you special, too. It isn't because you get to sit up front with your daddy; it's because your Daddy in heaven loves you very much and sent Jesus to die for your sins."

Lizzie fixed her gaze on Diana. "*Your* sins, too?"

Diana nodded. "Yes, honey. My sins, too."

Lizzie waited quietly for a moment then said, "I'm ready to go to sleep now, Mommy."

Diana smiled. "Good girl. You'll see Daddy tomorrow at breakfast. And when he does get home tonight, he'll come into your room and kiss you and whisper a prayer for you."

"He will?" The girl looked doubtful. "How do you know that?"

"Because he does that every night before he goes to bed."

The doubt melted away from her face, as Lizzie settled into her pillow and smiled. "I love you, Mommy."

Diana returned her smile. "I love you too, baby."

After a final hug and kiss, Diana turned out the light and left the room to wait for Paul.

By the time Paul finally turned into the driveway, he knew he hadn't made it home in time to see his children before they went to sleep. In fact, he wouldn't be surprised if Diana was asleep, too.

He pulled into the small, detached garage and turned off the engine. He had to admit that he preferred the spacious two-car garage they'd had in Port Mason to this one, but after what he'd witnessed in the past few hours, he dared not complain about anything.

He locked up the garage and went to the kitchen entrance to let himself in, taking off his shoes and carrying them so he could walk in his sock-clad feet as he made his way to the front of the house. If Diana was sleeping, he didn't want to disturb her.

All was quiet as he made his way down the hall, stopping at each of the children's rooms to look in on them, to pray, and to whisper goodnight before heading for his own room.

When he entered the master bedroom, he found Diana in bed, an open book lying on her chest. Paul smiled. His wife loved to read, but once she lay down, she never could stay awake long enough to finish even one chapter. Apparently tonight was no exception.

He made his way past the bed to his dresser in the corner where he took out a pair of clean pajamas and then turned to head to the bathroom down the hall.

"I'm not asleep," Diana murmured, her eyes fluttering open. "Well, not soundly anyway." She scooted up to a sitting position, leaned against the wooden headboard, and patted the bed beside her. "Come and tell me about it."

A pang of guilt pierced his heart. It was one thing to get called out at all hours to do the job you've promised to do, but something else entirely to break your word to your children and to awaken your wife who no doubt needed all the sleep she could get.

"Sorry," he said, settling down on the edge of the bed and laying a hand on hers. "I didn't mean to wake you."

Her half-smile warmed his heart. "I told you, I wasn't really asleep — just drifting in and out. So what happened? Is it something you can talk about?"

He considered her question then nodded. "With you, yes, though most of it will soon be common knowledge throughout town." He sighed. "That was Byron Phillips who called earlier. He had just received a call from his son, Max. He was at the police station . . . again."

Paul saw Diana's chest rise and fall as she took a deep breath. A look of compassion washed over her face. "I'm so sorry, sweetheart. I just don't know how poor Byron holds up under all this." She shook her head. "From what I understand, this is the third or fourth time his son's been arrested over the last year or so."

Paul nodded. "I'm afraid so. Thankfully nothing has been major enough to constitute a felony, at least not until now. But the officer Byron and I spoke to said they couldn't keep giving him a pass. He's not going to get off with a warning this time. He will definitely spend some time locked up."

Diana frowned. "So what did he do?"

"Well, his past arrests basically consisted of stealing something from Byron and hocking it. Since Byron couldn't bring himself to press charges against his own son, the police kept letting Max off with a stern reprimand." Paul shook his head. "This time he broke into the pawn shop where he'd previously hocked his dad's stuff. He didn't realize there was a silent alarm, so the police arrived in time to catch him trying to climb back out the way he'd come in . . . and with a bag of merchandise slung over his back. What makes it even worse is that the owner arrived before the police. He recognized Max and tried to wrestle the bag of merchandise away from him. In the struggle, he fell down and hit his head. It appears he's going to be OK, but it still makes for a tougher set of charges."

He heard Diana suck in her breath. "Uh-oh. That *is* worse — *much* worse. So what's going to happen to Max? Did Byron bail him out?"

"Yes. But he'll have to sign over his house to do it. You know Byron doesn't have much, especially since he went through his savings caring for his wife before she died. That house is just about all he has left." Paul ran his fingers through his hair. "I know that wasn't an easy choice, but we prayed about it together, and then I had to bow out and let Byron make the final decision."

Diana nodded and sighed. "That's all you could do, I know. It was undoubtedly a painful decision all the way around." She took her husband's hand in both of hers, squeezing gently. "So what happens next?"

"Since Max is only a few months short of his eighteenth birthday, he was booked as an adult. A public defender will meet with Max tomorrow, and then Max should be home with his dad by the end of the day." He shrugged. "That's all I know. I drove Byron home and prayed with him again, and then . . . Well, here I am."

He searched her eyes before he spoke again. "I am so very sorry about being out so late and missing time with the kids before they went to bed. From now on, I'm not going to make promises that I might not be able to keep."

Diana nodded. "I think that's wise. Now get ready for bed. I need to lie on your shoulder for a while."

Mitchell had awakened before dawn that Wednesday, and as usual, he wrapped himself in his robe and headed for his prayer closet. The little guest room was perfect for an extended visit with his Lord, and he began to pray even as he settled into the chair and picked up his Bible.

"Good morning, Father. I haven't peeked outside yet, but whatever the weather, I know it'll be a beautiful day. Thank you for letting me stay here another day, although You know I'd rather come home." He sighed. "I know, I know. Not yet. All right then. Where would You like me to read this morning? And as always, please let me know if there's someone in particular who needs prayer."

Drawn to Isaiah 43, he began to read aloud.

"But now, thus says the LORD, who created you, O Jacob, and He who formed you, O Israel: 'Fear not, for I have redeemed you; I have called *you* by your name; you *are* Mine. When you pass through the waters, I will be with you; and through the rivers, they shall not overflow you. When you walk through the fire, you shall not be burned, nor shall the flame scorch you.'"

Mitchell laid the precious book in his lap and leaned his head back against the chair, his eyes closed. "What is it, Lord? Are those words for me today . . . or is there someone else walking in fear right now that I should pray for?"

Though no names or faces came to mind, he sensed there was indeed someone else who needed to be covered in prayer that early morning. He didn't know who, but God did, and that was enough for Mitchell. He would stay in his chair and pray until he sensed the Lord's release to go and start his day.

Diana was stunned but pleasantly so. Paul had made a few phone calls when he first got up then announced at the breakfast table that his calendar was cleared for the morning.

"That means the three of us . . ." He nodded first toward Lizzie and then Micah. ". . . are going to do something very special."

As the impact of his words soaked in, the children lit up and hopped down from their chairs, bouncing up and down on their toes and squealing with delight as they hovered around Paul's chair.

"Where are we going?" Lizzie asked, nearly breathless.

Paul smiled as he laid a hand on each child's shoulders. "Settle down a little, and I'll give you a big hint."

Wide-eyed, with faces shining, they managed to stop bouncing. "What is it?" Lizzie demanded.

"Yeah, what is it?" Micah chimed in.

"Let's just say it involves pumpkins and hay and . . ." He paused a moment, his brown eyes twinkling as he looked from one child to the other then back again. ". . . and horses."

"Horses!" they screamed almost simultaneously as the bouncing and squealing started again.

Paul looked over their heads to Diana, his eyebrows raised. "Do you think you can find something to do while we're gone?"

For just a brief moment, Diana considered jumping up from her chair and running around the table to join Lizzie and Micah in their exuberance. But she managed to contain her excitement at the prospect of an entire morning on her own, something she hadn't really been able to do since pulling the children out of preschool. "I believe I can, yes," she answered, hoping Paul could read between the lines to know how much she appreciated this gesture on his part, particularly since it was Wednesday and he usually spent the day going over his notes for the midweek service that evening.

"Somehow I thought so." Paul returned his attention to the children. "All right, then. Just as soon as you two finish breakfast and get dressed, we're outta here!"

With no further prompting, Lizzie and Micah scrambled back to their seats and began wolfing down their oatmeal. Diana chuckled as Paul's eyes once more met hers. Then she picked up her spoon to finish her own breakfast. She didn't want to miss one moment of her husband's gift to her.

It wasn't difficult to decide where to go shopping in Desert Sands, as there was only one mall, and that mall had only one floor. Still, it contained most of the basic shops and a food court, so it suited Diana's purpose just fine.

I don't really need anything, she reminded herself. *Still, how often do I get a chance to take my time window shopping and strolling along? I usually have two children tugging on my hands wanting to go to the play area or eat ice cream.* Thankfully she could avoid those very places today.

She smiled at the thought of Paul and the children taking a hayride through the pumpkin patch. They attended a harvest festival at their previous church. Paul mentioned having something similar at Desert Sands Community, but Diana had argued that the congregation was too small to expect much of a turnout.

"It's not just for the congregation," Paul had reminded her. "It's for the rest of the community, too. That's why we call ourselves Desert Sands *Community* Church. If we decorate nicely and provide games and goodies for the kids, we just might bring in some new people from the neighborhood. After all, there hasn't been an active church in this immediate area for quite some time now."

She'd nodded, knowing he was right. And now, nearing the end of October, the mall was covered in harvest decorations. Maybe she'd find something they could use for their church harvest party.

With that in mind, she decided to keep her eyes open as she made her way down one side of the mall and then up the other. But she didn't get far before she stopped in her tracks, her eyes growing wide at the window display of a well-known department store.

Christmas decorations? Now? She was incredulous. *And with Thanksgiving still a month away?* She shook her head. The obvious commercialism of her favorite holiday threatened to dampen her joy at having the luxury of a morning to herself.

Diana sighed, halfheartedly fighting the heaviness that so often showed up and threatened her mood. "No," she said aloud, feeling determination rise inside her. "I won't give in to it. No one's going to steal my joy!"

A chuckle behind her caused her to turn her head. A woman with white hair stood smiling at her — Virginia Lopez.

"I don't know who's trying to steal your joy," Virginia said, her warm brown eyes twinkling, "but I'm glad you aren't going to let it happen." She leaned closer. "Sometimes we have to fight to hang on to joy. But trust me. It's worth it!"

After a few minutes of chitchat, Virginia started to leave then stopped suddenly and turned back. "I almost forgot," she said. "Please thank your husband for the tape player and cassettes of the Bible he brought to me. When my eyes get tired and can't keep reading, I just turn one of them on and listen to the beauty of God's Word." She smiled, her eyes sparkling. "It's one of the nicest gifts anyone has ever given me."

She turned again and proceeded on her way, leaving Diana staring at the retreating woman.

"Thank You, Lord," she whispered. "I know you sent that dear woman along just when I needed to hear what she had to say — and to see her grateful spirit."

She resumed her walk around the mall, determined to enjoy every remaining minute of her morning.

From the time Diana got home, slightly before noon, it had been full-steam ahead. She had soup and sandwiches made and on the table by the time her family returned, the kids chattering excitedly about the hayride, the horses, and who got the best pumpkin.

Paul glanced at Diana over the top of the children's heads then smiled and winked. "All right," he said, raising his voice just enough to be heard, "let's go wash our hands and then come and sit down for lunch. Then you can take turns telling Mommy about our morning."

Diana returned his smile, grateful that he seemed to understand her need for just a few more moments of peace. It hadn't lasted long, but neither did it take long for her to get caught up in their story of what truly did sound like a fun outing. She was still feeling grateful that evening when she and the children made their way to the church's front entrance, about 15 minutes before the midweek service would begin.

Paul had gone ahead of them an hour earlier. He would be spending the last few minutes in his office, praying before the service began, so Diana steered the children straight toward the children's rooms downstairs.

She flipped on the lights in the hallway as they proceeded to their room. Many rooms stood empty — as they often did, not just on Wednesdays, but on Sundays, too.

Five children, she mused. *Only five children who come regularly, and two of them are mine. We don't even have enough to divide them up by age.*

She sighed, telling herself to make the best of it, but she never set foot in the old building without thinking of how cheerful and roomy — and full! — their previous church had been.

No. She shook her head. *Don't even go there. Not again. No comparisons!*

Diana flipped on the light for the room where the children met on Wednesday evenings. Somehow she'd ended up leading the small midweek group, which included ages between three and eight. She refused to let herself think how bored the older couple of children must be because she had to simplify the lesson for the younger ones.

Maybe someday . . . these rooms will be full of children learning about Jesus.

How many times had those words danced their way through her mind, teasing her with hope she doubted would actually materialize?

Too many, she told herself, feeling guilty yet again. She shook away the thought and handed Lizzie an eraser then asked her to clean the small chalkboard in the front of the room. "And do it neatly," she cautioned.

No doubt feeling slighted, Micah called out, "I want to help!" He crossed the room and stood beside his sister before Diana could think of something else for him to do.

She sighed. "All right. Here's another eraser. You do the bottom half, Micah, and Lizzie can do the top."

Micah's lower lip came out. "I want to do the top. I'm big enough!"

Diana knew that wasn't true, but she also knew better than to tell her son otherwise. "I'm sure you are, Micah. You are both really good helpers, and I appreciate it very much. But I really need you to do a good job on the bottom half of the chalkboard while Lizzie does the top. We'll get done a lot faster that way. Now let's get to work — and no arguing!"

She pulled the half-page of notes she'd prepared for sharing the story of David finding King Saul in the cave but letting him go, even though Saul had been trying to kill David. She hoped to help the children understand how the Lord's words in Romans 12 — "Vengeance is Mine" — applied to them today. She would stress the need to forgive as God forgives, to not hold grudges, and to allow God to deal with seemingly unfair people or situations rather than trying to do it ourselves. She would pull it together with Jesus' instructions in Matthew 5:44 to pray for others — even those who hurt us — then end the class with a prayer circle.

As she finished laying out pencils and paper on the small round table where they'd all sit during the lesson, she heard children's voices drawing near. She smiled. *Good. At least the regulars will be here.*

Before she could step to the doorway to welcome the other children, a squabble broke out behind her. She turned in time to see Lizzie and Micah throwing the erasers at one another. Chalk dust filled the air, much of it landing on the children.

She sighed. Next time she'd plan ahead so they could each "help" at opposite ends of the classroom.

CHAPTER 9

Diana awoke early on Thursday morning. The light in the bedroom windows was just beginning to displace the darkness as Paul slept peacefully beside her.

She sighed and stretched, luxuriating in the rare quiet time before everything came to life. The thought flitted through her mind that she should put the time to good use by slipping out to the kitchen with her Bible and prayer journal. A twinge of guilt squeezed her heart as she realized how much she'd neglected that daily practice since leaving Port Mason. In her own defense, she reminded herself how much busier her life had become during her six months in Desert Sands. She also rationalized that there was no point in getting up to spend time in prayer when it was just a matter of moments before Paul would awake, and she'd have to put the coffee on and start planning breakfast while he showered.

As if to prove her point, Paul stirred. She didn't think he'd awakened to the alarm more than a dozen times throughout their marriage. He simply woke up "with the chickens," as he liked to say. His routine seldom varied. Wake up, take a shower and get dressed, pour a cup of coffee, and go outside to sit on the porch while he read his Bible and prayed. There were times Diana resented her husband's ability and discipline to keep a schedule, but then his full-time job wasn't to monitor two rambunctious children.

A faint memory, one without a name or shape but one that had been hanging around more often lately, teased her mind, causing her heart rate to jump up and goose bumps to crawl up her arms.

"A penny for your thoughts."

She shook off the unnamed feeling and took a closer look at her husband. There, in the growing light, she saw his eyes open wide. As they made that visual connection, he smiled.

"How is it possible that you wake up looking as beautiful as when you go to bed?" He reached up and put an arm around her, drawing her near.

She felt her cheeks grow warm. "I'm sure that's not true. I've seen my hair in the morning, not to mention my face sans makeup."

"I love your blonde curls going in every direction. And with those beautiful blue-green eyes and perfect skin, you do *not* need makeup."

She gave up further argument and settled into the crook of his arm, her head on his chest. Once again, his steady heartbeat reassured her.

"So what's on your calendar today?" she asked. "Anything unusual?"

She heard her husband's deep sigh before he spoke. "I'm going to meet Byron Phillips for coffee. He called yesterday and said he had an update on his son's situation, but he'd rather discuss it with me in person."

"I'd almost forgotten about that," Diana admitted, feeling yet another stab of guilt. "His son's name is Max, right?"

She felt Paul give a brief nod of affirmation. "From what I understand, Byron and his late wife raised Max in a loving home and in church, but he started rebelling a few years ago. It's been a roller-coaster ride ever since."

"I can't even imagine." Her mind flashed to Lizzie and Micah as she tried to picture either of them rebelling and getting into trouble. They were just too small for her to pull up such a picture, but she knew that if they ever did, it would be her fault. If only she were a better witness to others, especially her children.

She pushed the thought away and said what she knew she should. "I'll be praying about your meeting with Byron. Please let me know if there's anything else I can do."

Before Paul could answer, the alarm began to buzz. It was time to start another day.

As Diana waited for the coffee to be done and for her husband to come, freshly showered and dressed, she did her best to spend the time in prayer, particularly since she'd told Paul she'd pray for the situation with Byron and his son. Once he had his coffee and had gone outside to read and pray, she'd get her own quick shower before the children woke up wanting breakfast. But try as she might, she simply couldn't seem to keep her mind on prayer when the jumble of the new day already demanded her attention.

"That coffee smells wonderful," Paul said as he stepped into the kitchen. He smiled and planted a kiss on her forehead before taking the full cup she offered him. "Have time to join me outside?"

She hesitated then shook her head. "I wish I could, but you know the kids will be up any minute, and if I'm going to get a shower today, I'd better grab it while I can."

A hint of regret flashed through Paul's eyes, but he nodded. "Of course. If they wake up before you're done, I'll head them off at the pass."

She gave a half-smile at her husband's attempt at levity then headed toward the bathroom. She hadn't even set foot in the hallway when the phone rang. Her first thought was that it wasn't good news. Why else would someone call before eight in the morning?

"Hello?" Her husband's warm greeting flowed out of the kitchen doorway in her direction. "Mark, what a nice surprise! How are you?"

The answer seemed to take longer than Diana would have expected, reinforcing her suspicion that it wasn't good news — particularly when it came from the senior pastor of their former church. She returned to the kitchen door to better hear her husband's part of the conversation.

"Oh, I'm sorry to hear that. What happened?"

Another pause. Then, "I see. And you're right, of course. At her age, it's not too surprising, I suppose. And it's not surprising at all to God. He numbers our days, and He's granted quite a few to Alice. I know she's rejoicing with Him now, but what about her family?"

Again Diana waited, as tears threatened her eyes. As best she could figure, an elderly woman named Alice had passed away. She knew only one elderly woman at Dayspring named Alice, though certainly there could be others, particularly those who might have come since Paul and Diana had moved away. But the knot that was growing in the pit of her stomach nearly assured her of the woman's identity.

As Paul wound up the conversation, thanking Pastor Mark for the phone call and making a request to know about the service as soon as it was arranged, Diana drew near to her husband. When he hung up the phone, he turned to her and said, "Did you hear? Alice Boswell passed away last night — in her sleep. Her neighbor found her not more than an hour ago, when she went to check on her. I guess the two of them had a standing coffee date every morning and never missed without a phone call." He sighed and took Diana's arms in his hands. "Another precious saint of God, gone home to be with her Savior."

Diana knew she should focus on that wonderful truth, but the only thought that rolled through her heart and mind, crashing into her every emotion, was that Diana hadn't made time to drive back to Port Mason at least once to spend the afternoon with Alice in her lovely little garden. The two had discussed that very thing before Paul and Diana moved, and Diana had promised to do that "soon." Now *soon* had come and gone, and Diana wouldn't be able to make good on her promise.

Hot tears overflowed her eyes and spilled onto her cheeks, as Paul pulled her close and stroked her hair.

Paul was just returning to the church after his coffee meeting with Byron Phillips. His heart was heavy, though he knew God held the situation in His very capable hands. Byron had told him the public defender believed Max could very well be convicted of breaking and entering and might do some prison time. Paul couldn't help but wonder if he'd hold up as well as Byron seemed to be doing if one day it were Lizzie or Micah in trouble with the law.

"Pastor Paul!"

The greeting came from the parking lot, behind him. He turned and spotted Mitchell Green stepping out of his trusty old blue pickup. Paul realized he'd been so preoccupied that he hadn't noticed the other vehicle pulling into the lot. Though 20 or even 30 vehicles dotted the front of the lot each Sunday morning, with about half that number on Wednesday evenings, the parking lot was normally empty on weekdays. His own five-year-old Corolla was in the lot now only because he'd driven it to his meeting with Byron. He imagined that if he took the car back to his house, the children would think he was home for lunch and demand that he stay. He simply had too much work waiting for him in his office. He'd go home for lunch in a couple of hours, after he'd made a dent in his to-do list.

But now Mitchell Green was heading in his direction, his ever-present smile a warm contrast to the pain Paul had witnessed in Byron's eyes. Mitchell was a true pillar of the congregation, one who'd been an active member before the church moved, and had happily moved right back with it when he heard the building would once again be hosting a church family.

"Pastor," Mitchell repeated as he drew up in front of Paul and offered his right hand, "I'm so glad you're here. Do you have time to talk with me for a few minutes?"

Paul took the man's outstretched hand. "Of course. Come on in. I'm afraid I don't have any coffee to offer you. I just came back from a meeting, and I've already consumed a lot more caffeine than I should have. But, I'm happy to make a pot, if you'd like."

Mitchell chuckled as they walked down a hallway to the right of the sanctuary. "I know the feeling. I've done that more than once myself. I'm just fine, thank you."

Paul flipped the switch and lit up his spacious but comfortable office. "Have a seat," he offered, gesturing toward one of the two cushioned chairs in front of his desk. "What about some water?"

Mitchell shook his head and waved away the offer as he took his seat. "I'm fine. Really, Pastor. I just . . ." His smile faded only slightly as his rheumy eyes studied him from under bushy brows. "I've had something on my heart for a while now, and I thought it was about time I came and talked to you about it . . . since it involves you and your family."

The man had his attention now. Paul, who had already taken a seat behind his desk, sat forward just a bit. He waited for the man to continue.

Mitchell leaned forward, too, as if he needed to close the distance between them before making a connection. "I often get up during the night to pray, or spend several hours each day in my prayer closet, praying for all sorts of things the Father lays on my heart."

Paul nodded. He tried to do the same, but he imagined Mr. Green was more faithful about it than he.

"One of those topics of prayer is you and your family — as it should be, of course. One should always pray for the pastoral staff and their families. Don't you agree?"

"I certainly do. We need it."

"Exactly. Anyway, for the past few weeks, my burden to pray for your wife has been especially heavy. Am I being too forward in saying this?"

"Not at all," Paul assured him, though an unnamed concern began to niggle at his heart.

"Thank you." He took a deep breath then continued. "Since I'm already praying for you and your family almost daily now, I thought it best to alert you to that fact and to let you know that if you — or your wife, for that matter — ever have something specific you'd like me to pray about, I'd be more than happy to do so. Not that I want or need to know any personal details, of course, but maybe just a general topic or concern."

Mitchell paused then, and Paul realized the man was waiting for him to take the conversation from there. In that quiet moment, Paul remembered that though he still had a few people from Dayspring — including the ones who originally came with him to help replant Desert Sands Community — who he knew prayed for him regularly, he didn't really have another man that he could pray with and for regularly. It was something he knew Pastor Mark maintained on a regular basis, since Paul had been one of that close-knit trio before he moved. Perhaps this was God's way of saying he needed to establish that same practice with Mitchell.

"I'm humbled," Paul said, "as I always am when someone tells me they're praying for me or my family. It means a lot. What would you think about praying together now and asking God what He wants us to do here?"

Mitchell nodded, a wisp of gray hair falling forward onto his forehead. "I'd like that very much, Pastor. I truly would."

Paul got up from his chair and moved to the one next to Mitchell's. He reached out, and Mitchell took his hands. They closed their eyes and bowed their heads . . . and began to seek God together.

CHAPTER 10

More than a week had come and gone since Paul first received the news of Alice Boswell's home-going. It was Saturday morning, and he and the family had just hit the road for the drive to Port Mason. Normally it was a trip they all looked forward to, as they visited friends and places they'd enjoyed when living there. But this occasion had a somber overtone. The children would be dropped off with close family friends where they would play with three other young children, freeing up Paul and Diana to attend the memorial service.

Paul chanced a peek at Diana, who stared out the windshield, making it difficult to read her mood. However, Paul had noticed her close to tears on several occasions since they'd received the news about Alice. He knew Diana had considered Alice a friend, so it wasn't unusual that the older woman's passing might affect her. *Still,* Paul reasoned, *she knows Alice is with the Lord and we'll all see each other again one day. Why is she taking it so hard?*

There was only one answer. Alice's death stirred up all the feelings Diana had about their move from Port Mason, feelings Paul knew she tried to hide. He was going to have to be more considerate of his wife in the next few days, as she no doubt needed a little extra TLC. Besides, he couldn't risk letting regret or resentment build a rift between them.

Paul's mind drifted to a few weeks after he'd told Diana about their pending move. It was obvious from the time he first made his announcement that Diana had misgivings about leaving Port Mason.

But that was natural, wasn't it? It was where they'd lived through-out their seven years of marriage, where they'd watched their infant daughter and son grow into healthy toddlers and then preschoolers. It was where Diana had connected with the other women in the church, where she'd loved her home — which she had redecorated almost entirely by herself — and where she could go to the beach nearly any-time she wished.

Paul also knew his wife wanted to please the Lord, which included respecting her husband. He had watched her closely during the weeks between his announcement and their actual move. He'd seen her brush away tears more than once, but each time he'd try to talk with her about her feelings, her expression had brightened, and she'd assured him she was just fine. He'd finally resolved to take that statement at face value, at least until she was ready to talk about it. Now, today, he wondered if she'd ever be ready. He certainly couldn't fault her for not wholeheartedly supporting him in this new venture, at least not right away, but he doubted she was even close to being onboard with it, even now.

After a relatively quiet trip, due to the fact that Lizzie and Micah had napped most of the way, they arrived in Port Mason and dropped off the children. When they were back in the car alone, before he started the engine and with only a few blocks to the church, Paul once more glanced at his wife's silhouette.

"You doing OK?" he asked.

Diana started, as if she'd been somewhere far away. She blinked and turned to look at him. He watched the emotions dance across her face, beginning with surprise, interspersed with loss, and ending in a smile.

"I'm fine," she insisted. "How about you? Are you ready for your part in Alice's service? Did you have time to go over what you'd say today?"

"I did — on the way over here, actually." He smiled. "I'll just be speaking for about ten minutes. Pastor Mark will do the rest."

Diana nodded. "Yes. And I'm glad you'll be involved. Pastor Mark may have been her senior pastor for many years, but she always seemed to warm up to you."

Paul shrugged. "That's probably because I taught her senior adult Sunday School class for several years. She never missed a day."

"No, she didn't," Diana agreed, her lips forming a smile but the tone of her voice denying it. "Anyway, that's why I didn't talk much on the way over here. I knew you were thinking about what you'd say."

Paul started the engine then backed out of the driveway. As much as he tried to deny it, he knew Diana wasn't being completely truthful with him about why she'd been silent on the way over. Perhaps she really had wanted to give him time to think about his part in Alice's memorial, but he knew there was more.

He sighed as he steered the gray Toyota down the street, his mind flashing to his most recent prayer time with Mitchell Green. *Thank You, Lord, for bringing Mitchell alongside to pray for us. Please help Diana, Lord, and please . . . help me know what I can do to help her.*

The children were once again dozing off in the backseat as the Michaelson family retraced their route back home. The very thought of "home" pierced Diana's heart, but she refused to give in to the sadness that tempted her as they left Port Mason in their rearview mirror.

She sighed as she turned her head to peek at Lizzie and Micah. *Even my little ones have adjusted, Father. Look at them. They were happy to come here, but they're just as happy to go home. When we picked them up, they couldn't stop chattering about how much fun they had—and now they're sleeping soundly. What a simple transition all this has been for them.*

Realistically she knew the children had been excited about playing with friends they hadn't seen in a while, but she too had spent time interacting with old friends, and she didn't feel excited at all. In fact, if anything, she had a growing sense of unease, as if there were more to their recent move than she realized.

She turned her head back to stare out the window. The weather was gray and damp, but even if the day had been sunny and warm, she doubted her mood would have improved much. The problem wasn't the weather or the people she missed or the home she'd left behind. The problem was her. Period. She knew that, but what was she to do about it? And why did she feel so reluctant to probe what she knew was an uncertain fear related to the move?

I have to put this thing to rest, she told herself, turning toward her husband who'd been rather quiet since they'd started their homeward journey. "I thought the service was lovely, didn't you?" Before he could answer, she laid a hand on his arm. "Especially what you had to say. It was easy to see you knew Alice well. She would have enjoyed what you said about her."

Paul gave her a glance and a smile. "Thanks. Of course, it wasn't exactly hard to come up with something to say about a woman like Alice. Her love for the Lord spoke volumes to anyone who met her."

A woman like Alice. Would she ever be that kind of woman?

"That's true. And I imagine that had something to do with the huge turnout. It was quite a memorial service, with so many people sharing a favorite memory about Alice." She didn't mention how her heart nearly broke when one lady shared how Alice had been famous for her homemade soup and always seemed to show up on someone's doorstep with a pot of it just when it was needed most. Diana had been the recipient of that delicious soup more than once.

"Do you think Mark let it go on too long?" Paul asked, pulling her thoughts back to the present. "Not being on staff at Dayspring anymore, I didn't feel right in winding things up sooner."

Diana shook her head. "No, you're right. Pastor Mark was in charge. And honestly, I don't think it was too long. Alice was well loved, and people needed the chance to say something about her."

When Paul nodded but said no more, she reverted to staring out the window. Though the number of trees diminished as they drove, it was easy to see that autumn was in full swing. Thanksgiving was only a couple of weeks away, evidenced by the brilliant splashes of red and gold that caught her eye, but even that beauty didn't seem to fuel the joy in her that it once did.

Nothing does, and I don't know what to do about it. Help me, Father, please. I'm homesick, and I just can't make that go away.

Byron Phillips's rusty red pickup was parked in the otherwise empty church lot. Upon seeing it, Paul and Diana exchanged a wordless glance. He knew she understood he would have to go back to the church after dropping his family off at home.

He was glad he did, though he would have preferred to spend what was left of the day with his wife and children. But he'd known, even before Byron opened the door and stepped out of his truck, that something was seriously wrong.

In moments the two men were seated across the desk from one another in Paul's office. Paul had offered to make coffee, but Byron shook his head. "No, thanks, Pastor. I can't eat or drink . . . or even sleep." His red-rimmed eyes confirmed his words.

Paul didn't want to push Byron, but it was obvious the man's news wasn't good. Paul prayed silently while he waited for Byron to continue.

"He's gone," he said at last, resting his elbows on his knees and dropping his head into his hands. "Max . . . jumped bail."

The possibility had already flitted through Paul's mind, but he'd hoped and prayed it wasn't so. The ramifications began to unwrap themselves in Paul's thoughts as he prayed for wisdom.

"When?" he asked.

Byron raised his head, his face etched with lines that hadn't been there before. "Last night. But I didn't know it until this morning when I got up and went into the kitchen to make coffee. I . . . I found a note by the coffee pot."

Paul's heart sank. He'd been holding on to a sliver of hope that maybe Byron was wrong. Maybe Max had just gone for a long walk . . . or something. "Have you told anyone else yet?"

Byron shook his head. "No. I came here first. Even though you weren't here, I waited. I knew you'd get here sooner or later. And . . . I had nowhere else to go."

Tears stung Paul's eyes as he searched for something to say. Even after being in various areas of ministry for nearly two decades, he still felt inadequate at times like this.

"What did the note say?"

Byron opened his mouth and seemed to struggle to find the words. At last he sighed and began to speak.

"He said he loved me and always would. That he appreciated everything I'd ever done for him. But he just couldn't stick around and let himself end up in prison. He knew that's what it meant this time, so he . . . ran." Byron shook his head again. "He also said he was sorry about the house. *My* house. It'll belong to the bank soon."

Byron's house was small, a two-bedroom home in the older part of town that Byron and his wife had bought soon after they were married. Byron had told Paul about how they'd been about to sell it and move to a larger one when Byron's wife found out she had cancer.

After that, every spare dime they could scrape up went toward her treatment — sadly, to no avail.

It was one of those times when Paul felt at a loss for words. He knew he needed to comfort Byron, but what do you say to a man who's lost his wife and whose only child has turned to crime? And now Byron might very well lose his home. How do you encourage someone in that situation?

Paul left his chair and went around to the front of the desk, sitting down next to Byron. "I'm so sorry," he said. "Can we pray together?"

Byron's eyes flooded with tears, and he nodded. "Yes . . . please. I don't know what else to do."

Diana spent the morning telling the Thanksgiving story to Lizzie and Micah. Now they were busy coloring paper turkeys to display on the table. She'd planned to help them cut out the turkeys before they colored them, but Lizzie had announced that she could cut out her own. Micah then said he could, too. So with two sets of children's scissors and close oversight, she had allowed it. Micah's turkey looked more than a little misshapen, but both children seemed pleased as they worked on their projects.

She was busy preparing a simple lunch of grilled cheese sandwiches and soup, something to warm them on this cool autumn morning, when the phone rang. Her heart skipped a beat when she saw the name and number light up on caller ID.

"Megan? Hi! What a nice surprise. How are you?"

"I'm fine. How about you?"

Diana smiled. "Better now that I've heard your voice."

After a slight pause, Megan responded. "Is something wrong?"

Diana felt her face flush. She hadn't meant to intimate that she had a problem, and truthfully she didn't — other than her ongoing homesickness.

"No, no, not at all. We're . . . fine. The kids and I are just finishing up our morning lesson on Thanksgiving, and then we'll have lunch. What about you? What's going on in your beautiful corner of the world?"

Megan chuckled. "Beautiful as ever. You're right about that! It's a bit chilly this morning, but I imagine not as much as where you are.

I remember being out your way in the winter months, and it can get downright cold."

Diana sighed. "That's for sure. But it's a welcome relief from the sweltering heat we endured this summer. I'm so glad that's behind us until next year." She frowned. "So really, Meg, what's up? I was so disappointed that we didn't have time to really talk after Alice's service. Do you have a specific reason for calling, or did you just miss me?"

Megan chuckled again. "Yes to both. I do miss you. You know that, right? But I also have a specific reason for calling. You said you just finished your lesson with the kids about Thanksgiving. Well, that's why I called. I've been thinking about Thanksgiving, and I wondered if you and Paul and the kids would like to come here for the day. If you don't already have plans, that is . . ."

The invitation felt like a fresh infilling of hope and excitement in her heart, and Diana found herself nodding even before she spoke. "Yes, of course, we'd love that! We haven't made any plans, and sharing that day with you and your family sounds perfect. What can I bring? Or should I just come early and help you cook? Paul and the kids could come later."

"Seriously? Oh, Diana, that sounds perfect! Yes, let's plan on that. You and I can spend the early part of the day cooking up a storm, and then we'll eat when your family gets here." Diana imagined the smile in Megan's voice as she added, "Besides, you know Paul and David will spend the afternoon watching football together. It'll be like old times."

Diana's heart twisted at the reminder of their "old times." Megan's invitation would give her back at least one full day of joy.

Before they could take the subject any further, Diana noticed the soup beginning to boil on the stove. She cradled the receiver on her shoulder as she turned down the flame and stirred the soup. "You're right. Just like 'old times,' for sure. All right, let me put it on my calendar, and we can figure out the details later. For now, I gotta run. Lunch is calling me."

With a final chuckle, Megan said good-bye. Diana held the phone in her hand for a moment before setting it down. At last she sighed and got back to the business at hand.

It had been a productive morning, but now Paul realized he was hungry. He locked up his office and the church then headed down the walkway toward home. He smiled, thinking how much he enjoyed working so close to home and having lunch with his family nearly every day.

He shivered as a cold wind stirred up the dry leaves below the few trees they had between the church and parsonage. *I hope Diana fixed something warm.*

Paul grinned as he thought of the almost regular and excited greeting he received each time he came home. And sure enough, the front door opened as he stepped up on the porch. Cries of "daddy" surrounded him, and he stooped down to hug his children.

"Look what I made," Lizzie said. "It's a turkey. Isn't it beautiful?"

Paul nodded. "Yes, it is. Very beautiful. Great job, Lizzie."

The girl beamed, and Paul thought how much Lizzie reminded him of his late mother.

"I made a turkey, too, Daddy."

Micah held his colorful paper up to Paul's eyes, forcing him to lean backward a little just to see it. *I'd better check on getting some reading glasses,* he told himself. *They say your eyes go at 40, and I'm almost there.*

Aloud he said, "Micah, that's great! Your colors are perfect."

The boy threw his arms around his father's neck, and Paul stood up with Micah in one arm. He took Lizzie's hand and steered them all back into the house and to the kitchen. Something smelled awfully good in there!

When he spotted Diana setting the table, her smile the warmest he'd seen in a while, he set Micah down and released Lizzie's hand. Then he went to his wife, took her in his arms, and kissed her. "You look happy today. Any special reason?"

She lifted her eyebrows. "Actually, yes, there is. Sit down and I'll tell you about it over lunch."

Diana had been anxiously waiting for the chance to tell Paul of their Thanksgiving plans. They hadn't yet gotten around to making any plans of their own, but the issue had been niggling its way into Diana's awareness for a couple of weeks now. Thanksgiving had always been one of her favorite holidays, and she'd loved their holiday get-togethers at Dayspring, particularly since her mother and stepfather lived too far away to visit regularly. She imagined the reason she hadn't brought up the subject before this was because it was too depressing for her to think of the four of them having their Thanksgiving celebration alone — not that they couldn't include some parishioners from Desert Sands, of course, but it just wouldn't be the same.

She took a deep breath and dove right in, eagerly anticipating her husband's pleasure at the unexpected invitation. "Megan Kellogg called a little while ago."

Holding his soupspoon midway between his bowl and his mouth, he lifted his eyebrows. "Really? Is everything all right?"

"Everything is better than all right — great even." She waited until Paul had swallowed his soup and their eyes reconnected. "She called to invite us for Thanksgiving."

The expected look of a pleasant surprise didn't materialize. Instead she watched as a slight frown formed above Paul's eyes.

"That's really nice of them," he said, setting his spoon down but keeping his eyes fixed on his wife. "I can see where that would be tempting, but . . ." His voice trailed off as his frown deepened. "You didn't accept, did you?"

Diana felt her eyes go wide. Didn't accept? Why in the world would he imagine that? "Of course I accepted," she said, feeling the strain of keeping her smile in place. "We love the Kelloggs, and it's not like we have other plans."

She waited, her heart rate rising as she watched an unreadable expression settle on Paul's face. A faint buzzing started in her ears, drowning out the children's occasional noises as they ate.

Paul's eyes darted to the children and then back to Diana. "Why don't we talk about this after lunch? Maybe while Lizzie and Micah are napping."

Diana followed her husband's example and glanced at the children before answering. They were dawdling over their food but had suddenly turned their full attention to their parents. One set of brown eyes and one of blue seemed to be studying her, waiting to hear her response to their father's words.

Before she could look away, Micah's face seemed to crumple and his lower lip came out. "I'm not a baby," he declared. "I don't want to take naps anymore."

"If I have to take one, so do you," Lizzie informed him.

"Do not!"

"Do too!"

"Enough," Paul said. "Finish your lunch, and then you can go lie down for a while, just like you always do. If you don't sleep, that's fine, but you know your mom needs some quiet time of her own every day. She'll come and get you up when it's time."

Nap time had recently been meeting with increased protests and resistance. However, once she had them down on their beds with a book or favorite toy, they nearly always dozed off. But that wasn't Diana's main concern at the moment.

After what seemed an eternity, Paul and Diana got Lizzie and Micah into their rooms and tucked into their beds

"So," Diana began as the two of them reentered the kitchen, "is there something I don't know about Thanksgiving?" She poured them each a cup of coffee and sat down across from her husband.

Paul took a deep breath as he raked his fingers through his hair. "Apparently there is," Paul answered, "though I'm afraid I assumed you'd realize we have an obligation to our congregation, even — and maybe especially — at holiday times. I guess we've never really talked through this before."

It was Diana's turn to frown. What in the world was he talking about? She opened her mouth to voice the question, but Paul jumped in ahead of her.

"Diana," he said, reaching across the table to cover her hand with his, "I know we have a small congregation, but some of them are alone for the holidays. Their church family is all they have. And just this morning..."

His voice trailed off, and Diana could see he was praying before he continued. "Just this morning I had a call from Virginia Lopez. She's feeling much better since her hospital stay, and she wanted to do something special for the holidays — for the 'shut-ins,' as she put it. But she also said it would be too much to have something at her home, and she wondered if we might host Thanksgiving dinner in the church fellowship hall. The kitchen is large and well-equipped, as you know, so we could do the main part of the cooking there. A couple of the women would come early to help you and Virginia cook, so it really wouldn't be that much work if — "

Diana interrupted before he could say another word. "Help me with the cooking? *Help* me? So you're saying I'd be in charge of everything that needs to be done in the kitchen. And have you thought of Lizzie and Micah? What am I supposed to do with them while I'm doing all this cooking?"

She knew her voice was becoming shrill, but she couldn't seem to bite back the words. "Were you even going to ask me about any of this before you committed me to it? Didn't it occur to you that I might have plans, too?"

Paul's face slackened, and he dropped his eyes a moment before responding to her many questions. "You wouldn't be doing everything in the kitchen, Diana. I told you, others will be there to help with whatever needs to be done. You'll just be coordinating that part of it — finding out who's coming and assigning them something to bring if they can, that sort of thing. And don't worry, someone else will clean up. As for Lizzie and Micah, Virginia's niece has already offered to keep an eye on them and any other children who come before dinner is ready. She'll keep them in one of the children's church rooms. They love it there, so it's not a problem."

Not a problem? Was he kidding? She did her best to keep her voice calm, but she knew she wasn't achieving the desired results. "How can you say it won't be a problem? Didn't you hear what I said — that I might have plans, too? I know I should have waited and talked to you before accepting Megan's invitation, but I couldn't imagine you'd have any objections." She took a deep breath. "Thanksgiving in Port Mason with David and Megan and their family would be perfect. I offered to go early so she and I can cook together. You and the children could either come with me in the morning, or drive over later in time for dinner." She leaned over the table, even as she squeezed his hand and looked into his eyes. "Paul, can't we just put Virginia — or someone else — in charge? I don't see why we have to be there."

Paul's brown eyes darkened a bit, and Diana realized she'd hit a nerve. Would it be to her advantage? She hoped so, but at the same time doubted it.

"Diana, we came here to relaunch a church. I'm the senior pastor, and you're the pastor's wife. Right now we're too small for any support staff, so we're it. You and me. A team. Remember how we used to talk about that even before we got married? We also prayed about it, and I thought you were onboard with it." He paused then asked, "Was I wrong?"

Hot tears bit Diana's eyes, and she felt her heart twist in pain. Everything he was saying was true and right, but it didn't change the fact that she didn't want to be here. But in that moment, she knew they wouldn't be going to David and Megan's for Thanksgiving. They would be staying here in Desert Sands, hosting dinner for a handful of people who had nowhere else to go.

She pulled her hand away from Paul's and lifted her chin. "No, you're not wrong, Paul. You're right. We'll have Thanksgiving dinner in the fellowship hall. I'll call Megan this afternoon and cancel."

Paul didn't answer right away. When he did, he stood to his feet and came around to her side of the table to plant a kiss on top of her head. "Thank you, sweetheart. I knew you'd understand." He turned toward the door leading to the entryway, and Diana watched him start to walk away. After a few steps, he turned back. "I forgot to mention that Virginia suggested we invite a few homeless people for Thanksgiving dinner. Not an open invitation or anything, just a few who might not have anyplace else to go. But if you'd rather not do that part . . ."

Diana waved away his comment. "No problem. Just invite them." She forced a smile. "The more, the merrier, right?"

Paul returned her smile. "True. But I don't want to heap too much on you all at once. You think and pray about the homeless people part, and I'll tell Virginia we'll get back to her about it in a couple days. Fair enough?"

She nodded. "Sure. Fair enough."

Diana sat, silent and unmoving, long after the front door had closed behind Paul. It wasn't until she heard Micah calling from his room and saying he had to go to the bathroom that she finally moved. "Yes," she said, heading toward the hallway, "you can get up now."

Lizzie's door sprang open, and the child poked her head out, eyes round as she opened her mouth to speak.

"You too, Lizzie," Diana said, not waiting for her to voice her question.

The children came bouncing and chattering from their rooms, ready to start the next part of their day. She wished she had half of their energy and enthusiasm because at that very moment, she had none of either. How would she ever muster the energy to put together Thanksgiving at the church when she could hardly keep up with her two children?

A few hours later, as his workday came to an end, Paul heard a knock on his office door. He went to open it and found Virginia Lopez, a big smile lighting her face and a plastic sack full of what looked like groceries, along with her purse, hanging from her arm.

"Good afternoon, Pastor," she said, stepping inside as he backed up to give her room. "I know I didn't make an appointment, but I was on my way home from the market and thought I'd take a chance and stop by. I hope you don't mind."

"Not at all, Mrs. Lopez. Please . . . have a seat." He indicated the two seats in front of his desk as he returned to sit in the one behind it.

"Virginia. Remember?" She settled into one of the chairs, setting her groceries and purse on the floor beside her.

He hadn't remembered, but he did now. "Yes. Virginia, of course. It's nice to see you up and around. You must be feeling better."

She flashed a warm smile. "Oh, I am. Much better! I hate hospitals. I know I look my worst when I'm there."

Paul couldn't help but return her smile. She really was a dear lady, and he hoped she and Diana could become friends, despite the age difference.

"So how can I help you?" Paul asked, leaning back in his chair and clasping his hands behind his head.

"Actually, I'm hoping I can help you." She leaned forward, her brown eyes sparkling. "You know that talk we had this morning—

about inviting some homeless people to have dinner with us here on Thanksgiving?"

Paul nodded, even as a knot began to form in his stomach. He knew deep down that things hadn't been resolved with Diana — may not have been for some time now — and he couldn't help but wonder if this visit from Virginia would help or hinder that resolution.

"Well, I no sooner finished my conversation with you than my son called to check on me. While we were talking, he told me about a young family he met at the grocery store today. He got to talking with them, and he eventually realized they were homeless, stranded here in town on their way to look for work. All their earthly possessions are stored in their car — which, for now, isn't running."

She chuckled. "That son of mine! Albert has such a tender heart. Fortunately his wife, Karen, does too because he's always bringing somebody home for dinner — or more. This time Karen got quite a surprise when Albert showed up with a family in tow. They fixed them something to eat, and then Albert took Karen aside and asked if she'd mind having them stay a little while. They have plenty of room after all, what with my two granddaughters off at college. Anyway, this couple is going to be with them for a while — until Albert can help them find a place of their own."

She leaned back then, as if the confidential part of her story was done. Virginia smiled. "When I asked him if they had plans for Thanksgiving dinner, he said they'd probably just fix something there and have the little family join them — me too, of course." Her eyes lit up another notch. "So I told him about the Thanksgiving dinner we're having here at the church and how we were thinking it would be nice to invite a few homeless people to eat with us." She chuckled. "I could nearly hear him smiling through the phone. So there you have it. Isn't God amazing?"

Paul blinked. He certainly agreed that God was amazing, and he supposed this meant the homeless family would be their guests for Thanksgiving dinner. Now all he'd have to do is break the news to Diana. He only hoped she'd had time to absorb the original Thanksgiving news before he added to it.

Paul decided to wait until the children were in bed to break the news to his wife. There was a time he would have assumed she'd be as excited about such news as Virginia seemed in announcing it, but after Diana's reaction earlier in the day, Paul knew this wasn't the time to *assume* anything.

He glanced at his watch. 7:30. Dinner was over, and Lizzie and Micah had taken their baths and were told by Diana to pick up their toys and go to bed. As usual, they were dragging their feet at their mother's directions.

He stood up, ready to jump in and help Diana get the children moving and off to bed, when his cell phone rang. He pulled it from his pants pocket and looked at caller ID. Byron Phillips.

"Hello, Byron. Is everything all right?"

The man's voice sounded strangely heavy, yet relieved. "As all right as it can be, I guess." He paused. "It's about Max."

Paul had figured as much. "Any word?"

"He turned himself in a couple hours ago." He sighed. "I'm glad. I was worried about him getting hurt if he pushed a confrontation with the police."

Paul nodded, heaving a sigh of relief himself. He'd been concerned about the same thing. "So how did you find out, and what happens now?"

"I got a call from his public defender. He's going to meet with him in the morning. He said it isn't a good thing that Max took off like he did, but it should work in his favor that he turned himself in." Another sigh. "He also said I probably won't lose my house. We'll have to talk with the bail bondsman and see what we can work out, but the lawyer thinks we should be OK on that."

"Glad to hear it." He truly was. He'd wondered what would happen to Byron if he lost his home at his age. "I'll be praying about the entire situation, the house included."

"Thanks, Pastor. Anyway, I just wanted you to know what was going on. I'll call you tomorrow when I know more."

Paul thanked him and settled back down in his chair. It seemed Diana had things under control with the kids, and he wanted a few minutes to pray before helping to tuck them in for the night.

He bowed his head, ready to begin praying, when Diana came up behind him and laid a hand on his shoulder. He raised his head to look up at her.

"Everything all right?" she asked.

He nodded. "Max Phillips turned himself in."

Relief washed over Diana's face. "Thank God."

Paul nodded. "We'll know more tomorrow after the public defender's had time to meet with Max. Understandably he won't get out on bail again, but by turning himself in, he may have saved his father's house."

Diana smiled. "I'm glad. I know you were about to pray, so go ahead. Come in when you're done, and we'll put the kids to bed together."

Paul nodded. He also reminded himself to include another prayer for his wife, that she would receive the news about the homeless family without resentment.

Diana had mixed emotions as she and Paul finished tucking in the children then returned to the kitchen for a cup of tea. Diana knew Paul preferred coffee, but he went with tea in the evenings because he agreed that Diana was right about it being more relaxing.

As she filled the kettle and put it on to boil, she wondered which of them would be first to bring up the Thanksgiving issue. She'd wrestled with it most of the afternoon and had finally come to the conclusion that she would simply have to call Megan and cancel. She wanted to be a good wife to Paul and a good daughter to her Lord, and she recognized she couldn't do either if she continued to argue her case about Thanksgiving dinner. But she hadn't called Megan yet because she held on to a slim hope that Paul might tell her he'd changed his mind and they would go to Port Mason after all.

By the time the kettle began to whistle, Paul had joined her in the kitchen. He came up behind her and slid his arms around her waist as she poured the boiling water over the tea bags resting in the matching mugs.

"Long day?" he asked as he kissed the back of her neck.

She set the kettle back on the stove and turned toward Paul. She desperately wanted to ask him to please reconsider about Thanksgiving, but she bit back the words and promised herself she'd let him bring it up first.

"Somewhat," she answered, "but not much more than usual. How about you?"

"The same. Not much more than usual. I'm hoping Byron's call is the last until tomorrow."

Diana nodded and turned to retrieve the steaming mugs.

"I'll get those," Paul offered.

She flashed him a quick smile of gratitude and went to the table to sit down.

Paul set the mugs in front of them and joined her. She'd caught him looking at her several times throughout the evening, and she couldn't help but hope it was because he had realized how much it meant to her to have Thanksgiving dinner with friends.

She smiled. "I imagine everyone is relieved that Max is back home safely."

"Oh, he's not home. Running off like he did precludes that. Now he'll have to be in custody until the trial."

She nodded. She should have realized that. "Well, at least we know he's safe."

Paul smiled and reached out to cover her hand with his. "So . . . have you thought anymore about Thanksgiving? About how you and Virginia might work together to coordinate things? She's excited about doing it, but I think it would be too much for her alone." He squeezed her hand, still smiling. "It would be a great chance for you two to get to know each other."

Diana's heart twisted as her last hope for Thanksgiving in Port Mason faded away. She knew she needed to be gracious, to say something in response, but she couldn't seem to come up with the right words.

"It's only for one day," he said softly.

Only for one day? Didn't he realize it wasn't about how long it would take? It was about spending that particular day with friends in a community she still loved and missed. She forced a smile.

"I know. And that's fine. I'll . . . give her a call tomorrow or the next day."

Paul picked up her hand and kissed it. "Thank you. I know it'll all work out."

She nodded and sighed. "So how many do you think will come? Our congregation is small anyway, and I imagine most of them will want to have dinner with their families, rather than at the church."

"Virginia said she imagined we would have eight or ten, though she doesn't have an exact count yet. And then, of course, there's the homeless family —"

Paul stopped mid-sentence, and she knew he'd said something he wished he hadn't. But she wasn't about to let him get by without an explanation. "The homeless family? What are you talking about, Paul?"

She watched his Adam's apple slide up then down, and she knew he was squirming a bit. She waited.

"Virginia came by this afternoon and said she'd heard about a homeless family who might like to come to our dinner. You remember I mentioned the possibility of inviting some of the homeless, right?"

Diana nodded. She remembered, but she hadn't really thought it would happen. It seemed the day was taking on a life of its own, and she might as well surrender and go along for the ride.

"I'll talk to Virginia about it tomorrow. We'll figure it out."

Paul smiled, his relief obvious.

Before he could speak she stood up and looked down at him. "I'm sorry, sweetheart, but I'm really tired. I think I'll head to bed."

I t had been a long night but a productive one, he was sure. Mitchell Green had sensed the breakthrough just before morning light, and now he was sitting at his kitchen table sipping coffee, munching on toast.

"It was good to be with You through the night, Father. I'm so grateful You've given me a heart to pray." He chuckled. "I think we about ran the gamut of everyone at Desert Sands Community, didn't we?"

He took another sip of coffee. Though he'd spent the majority of the night praying for every individual and family from their small congregation, the most time was spent praying for their pastor and his family. *Which is as it should be. Pastors are blessed to be able to serve as they do, but it's not an easy life. So much is expected of them . . . and of their families.*

He glanced up at the kitchen clock. 6:30. Still early. Plenty of time to take care of the few things that needed doing before he went to the church to get together with Pastor Paul for their prayer time at 10:00.

Mitchell smiled. "Thanks for that too, Lord. I'm honored to serve as a prayer shield for our pastor and his family, not only like last night but also by getting together with him every week. But please remind me to ask if he'd pray for me, too. I've been so focused on hearing what he wants me to pray about for him and his family that I've forgotten to tell him about my own needs." He rubbed his arthritic hands together. "At my age, most of my needs are physical ones, problems that will go away once I breathe my last and come home to You." He shook his head. "Isn't that something? So many people spend their lives trying to find a way to outrun death, when all they need to do is turn to You and receive Your love and peace. Just knowing that I get to be with You when I leave here makes it hard not to want to go sooner."

He went to the stove and poured himself another cup of coffee from the old metal percolator he'd used for decades. He didn't have much use for all those newfangled gadgets that spit out coffee or tea or hot chocolate, one cup at a time, depending on your mood.

Just good old-fashioned strong java is all a man needs to get moving in the morning. I don't know how they can even call that stuff with all the whipped cream and spices on top "coffee."

He sat back down and opened his dog-eared Bible. "I read nearly all the way through the Psalms and Isaiah last night, Lord. What should I read this morning?"

Feeling prompted to turn to Ephesians, he did so and then settled in for some more reading before he got started on his day.

Paul had been apprehensive when he awoke. Diana had been asleep by the time he went to bed the night before, and now she was already up, so he had no idea what to expect.

But I prayed, Lord—long and hard. And I know You gave me a peace about it before I fell asleep. Help me to hang on to that peace today—and to love my wife as You love the church.

After he'd showered and dressed, he opened the bathroom door and stepped out into the hallway, where he was greeted with the tantalizing aroma of bacon frying. The grin on his face came automatically as he remembered telling Diana more than once that his favorite breakfast food was bacon and anything.

He was definitely feeling encouraged by the time he entered the kitchen. When he discovered his wife was making not only bacon but pancakes as well, it was all he could do not to pump his fist in the air and cry, "Thank You, Jesus!"

Instead he crossed the kitchen to where she stood turning bacon in the skillet. "Wow," he said, "is this some special occasion that I missed? This looks fantastic!"

She paused and turned her face toward his. Her smile seemed genuine. "I suppose it is. I realized during the night how petty I've been about the Thanksgiving thing. I'm sorry, and I wanted to do something nice for you."

He smiled. "Hence the bacon and pancakes."

She nodded and went back to fixing breakfast.

"Well, whatever the reason, thank you. Can I help?"

She paused. "Sure. You can set the table — and don't forget the butter and syrup."

Paul's grin broadened. "Don't worry. I won't. What's bacon and pancakes without a ton of butter and syrup?"

Her eyes twinkled when she glanced toward him. "Maybe a lot less fattening?"

He chuckled and went about setting the table for four, though he secretly hoped they might have a little time alone before the children joined them.

"I'm sorry for dumping all this Thanksgiving stuff on you," he said as he helped her carry a platter of pancakes and another one of bacon to the table.

"It's . . . all right," she said, but Paul couldn't help but notice the hesitation in her voice. "You are the pastor here after all, and I'm the pastor's wife. As such, we should both realize that certain things are required of us. I'll call Virginia today to get things started."

Paul nodded, pleased at the change in her attitude but saddened that it seemed she still saw the plans as some sort of chore. *She'll come around*, he told himself. *After all, she's already come a long way since last night. Thank You, Lord.*

As they sat down at the table beside one another and bowed their heads to offer thanks, Paul felt Diana's hand slip into his, bringing tears to his eyes. But he blinked them away, cleared his throat, and began to pray aloud.

Mitchell Green showed up at Paul's office, Bible in hand, at precisely 10 o'clock — the exact time they'd agreed upon, Paul recalled, though he'd forgotten about it until now. Fortunately he had nothing pressing before his meeting with the church board at 11:00.

He smiled at the thought. The church board at Desert Sands Community consisted of exactly two other people besides himself. One was Byron Phillips, who'd recently submitted his resignation because of what was going on with Max. The other was the nearly bald man with the dancing eyes who stood in front of him right now.

"So glad you're here, Mitchell," Paul said, extending his right arm to shake the man's hand then indicating the chairs across from him. "Sit down, please. Would you like some coffee? Won't take long to fix a pot."

Mitchell shook his head. "No thanks, Pastor. I've already passed my two-cup limit this morning."

Paul chuckled. "You and me both." He opted to sit in the chair next to Mitchell rather than the one behind his desk. This was about two brothers praying together, not about a pastor and parishioner dealing with some sort of personal or church-related issue.

Sitting next to his visitor, he pulled his chair around so the two could face one another. Mitchell did the same.

"It looks like we'll go right from our prayer meeting to the board meeting this morning," Paul announced. "And it'll only be you and me—enough for a quorum, so we can go ahead with it. Byron has resigned because of all he's going through with his son." He sighed. "That's one thing we'll really need to pray about this morning—a third board member. I hate to lose Byron, but I certainly understand his need to pull back for now."

Mitchell nodded. "Yes. I can only imagine how difficult it is. But when I was praying about the situation during the night, I got a real peace about it. Is there some update I don't know about?"

"Actually, yes, there is. As you know, Max had seemingly jumped bail. Not only was that a worry for Byron, as who knew what might happen to his son at that point, but Byron might have very well lost his home since he put it up for the bail. But you're right. Something did happen. Max turned himself in, and though his bail is revoked and he'll have to remain in custody while he awaits trial, it looks as if Byron won't lose the house."

"That *is* good news." Mitchell smiled. "No matter what we're going through or what pops up in the course of the day, God is good."

"All the time," Paul added, returning Mitchell's smile.

"So," Mitchell said, "shall we open in prayer and then spend some time in the Scriptures before getting down to serious intercession?"

"That sounds like a good plan to me," Paul said, bowing his head as he realized how grateful he was for this man of God who had offered himself to pray for his pastor and his family. *As well as everyone else in the church and beyond, I'm sure.*

D iana hung up the phone, a feeling of fluid warmth enveloping her.

I like Virginia Lopez, she admitted to herself. *Certainly more than I imagined I would. Maybe working with her on this Thanksgiving thing won't be so bad after all—even though I'd still rather be going to Megan's.* She sighed, remembering that when she called Megan to cancel, her friend had been completely gracious and understanding, saying they would take a rain check sometime between Thanksgiving and Christmas. When she mentioned it to Paul at lunch, he'd been more than agreeable. So she had that to look forward to.

She heard slight noises from down the hall, and she realized her children hadn't gone to sleep as she'd hoped. She glanced at her watch and decided she had just enough time to sit down and relax with a cup of coffee before it was time for the children to get up. She fixed the coffee, splurging by adding a touch of chocolate to it, then sat down at the kitchen table and put her feet up.

Her mind went immediately to the conversation she'd had with Virginia. They'd decided they needed to start this Thanksgiving project with at least one face-to-face meeting. After that they might be able to manage with phone meetings. Time would tell.

She sipped her coffee and closed her eyes as she savored the warmth and flavor. *Thank You, Lord. The coffee is absolutely delicious, and the house is* almost *absolutely quiet.* She smiled. The morning fog had burned off, and by the time Paul had come home for lunch, it had been warm enough to eat outside on the porch. She knew some sunshine still shone through the kitchen window behind her, so why not take advantage of a nearly perfect fall day? She'd get the children up when she finished her coffee, grab light jackets for all of them, and then go for an "exploring walk," something the kids loved to do. They'd each bring a small brown bag and fill it with odds and ends they discovered along the way — a special leaf or rock, a flower petal — anything that caught their eye and fit in the bag.

She took one last gulp of her coffee then got up and put the mug in the sink before heading down the hallway to tell her children about the planned outing. No doubt they'd be excited. It didn't take much to get them onboard with something they considered "fun."

It may not be a spontaneous trip to the beach, but I suppose it can still be nice, right, Lord?

She heard no response, but she could sense her Father's smile.

Paul wished he'd had the afternoon free so he could have joined his family on their "exploring walk." Diana had dropped by with the kids to let him know what they were doing, and Lizzie and Micah had begged him to come with them, but he needed to take care of some correspondence and start outlining his next sermon. The children were disappointed, but lit up again when he promised to bring them a surprise when he came home that evening.

He chuckled. Now he just needed to figure out what that surprise would be.

As he sat at his desk, his Bible open and his computer turned on and waiting, he found his mind drifting back to the office he'd occupied as a staff member at Dayspring. Though he wasn't the senior pastor there, his office was nearly as big as the one he sat in now. And it was certainly more modern.

He sighed. Though he'd enjoyed his duties as an associate pastor at Dayspring, his heart had longed to plant a church and to be its senior pastor. He had always loved the idea of taking on a congregation at fledgling status, and then nurturing it to a more mature level. In his mind he could see a younger version of himself and Diana, an engagement ring on her finger, as they talked about their future in ministry together. They'd prayed — more than once — and committed their lives to whatever God had planned for them. How had Diana let that vision slip away? How had she become so attached to Dayspring Church and her home and life in Port Mason that she'd not wanted to leave to follow God's call?

To be fair, she'd come along without outward complaint. And she'd done her best to adjust, even agreeing to give up Thanksgiving dinner with one of her best friends and instead work with Virginia to prepare a dinner for anyone in the congregation who wanted to come — as well as for people in the community who might join them, and yes, even a homeless family.

Paul shook his head. *And yet she's lost her joy, Lord. I see sparks of it on occasion, but overall, it's gone. I miss her dancing eyes and the bounce in her step. What can I do to bring it back, Father?*

Nothing.

Paul jerked upright in his seat. It wasn't often he heard the Lord speak to him audibly. This time it sure seemed that way, though it was most likely in his heart. Still, the answer was straightforward.

"You're right, Lord, of course," he said, his voice barely above a whisper. "I know our joy comes only from You. But I feel like I should do something as her husband to help her receive Your joy again."

Just love her . . . as I love the church. Leave the rest to Me.

Paul nodded. There was no doubt what God was telling him, nothing to analyze or discuss with someone else. His only command from the Lord regarding his wife was to love her as Christ loved the church — completely, unconditionally, and selflessly. It was a tall order.

All right, Lord. I'll commit to do that, but please help me. Apart from You, I can't love anyone that way. I just don't have it in me.

The voice spoke yet again to his heart. *You have My Spirit in You. You have My Word to read and meditate on. And you have Me right here, ready to help you anytime you need it. Am I not enough?*

Hot tears pricked Paul's eyes, and he slipped to his knees. Leaning his elbows on his chair, he clasped his hands and bowed his head. "You are enough, Lord. You're always enough. Forgive me for losing sight of that and trying to run off on my own to get things done — especially when it involves my family. They're only my family because You've loaned them to me. Ultimately, they're Yours. Oh, Lord, I need to learn to love them that way, to always be ready and able to say the Lord gives and the Lord takes away. Blessed be the name of the Lord . . ."

Bless Virginia for agreeing to come to the parsonage for their initial meeting about Thanksgiving. Diana was now able to schedule their meeting while the children were in their rooms napping — or playing, as the case may be. Taking them with her to Virginia's house would have been disastrous, as Diana never relaxed when she had the children at someone else's home — particularly someone Virginia's age whose children were all grown. She'd considered asking Virginia to meet her in the largest children's church room, where Lizzie and Micah could play, but even that opened too many possibilities for interruption and distraction.

Diana finished clearing the table of the lunch dishes, then rinsed them and stuck them in the dishwasher — one of the few fairly modern aspects of this otherwise outdated home. She purposely pushed away the memory of her brand new dishwasher, one she had chosen herself, sitting there in her spacious, sunny kitchen in Port Mason. This was no time to get stuck in memories. Virginia would be here in less than 15 minutes, if indeed she was as prompt and dependable as Paul insisted she was.

A giggle from one of the bedrooms reached her ears, and she stopped what she was doing to go check on her children. Lizzie lay quietly on her bed, looking through one of her favorite early-reader books. Micah, on the other hand, was stacking blocks as high as he could, laughing when they came tumbling down. As soon as he saw his mother standing in the open doorway to his room, he set his blocks down and returned to his bed.

"Books or quiet toys only, remember? And only in bed."

His lower lip protruding slightly, Micah nodded. Then he raised a pitiful looking face and said, "I love you, Mommy."

Diana was caught between a laugh and a softening heart that said, "Go ahead and play with whatever you want." But she managed to block both reactions.

"I love you too, Micah. Now Mommy has things to do in the kitchen. Then I told you I have a friend coming over, right?"

Micah nodded, his blond curls and big blue eyes helping to maintain the baby look she so loved about him. But he wasn't a baby, and she needed him to mind.

"All right. I'm going back to the kitchen now. Will you promise to stay on your bed and play quietly until I call you to come out?"

The boy nodded again, and though she first resisted the urge, she then gave in to it and quickly crossed the room and bent down to give Micah a kiss on his forehead.

The boy's smile was radiant. "Will you pray with me, Mommy?"

She always said Micah knew exactly how to get to her, and this was no exception. How could she possibly ignore such a request? And so, despite the fact that she'd prayed with each child when she put them down just minutes earlier, she uttered a short prayer with her son then left the room to finish preparing for her visitor.

CHAPTER 15

If Diana thought the run-up to Thanksgiving would be relatively peaceful, she was wrong. Lizzie caught a cold and shared it with Micah, then Micah fell off his tricycle and scraped his knees and the palms of his hands. Diana had to watch him constantly to be sure he didn't pick off the scabs while he healed.

But now Thanksgiving had finally arrived. Paul had planned to stay with the children while Diana was busy cooking, but then he'd been called out on another hospital visit, this time to a relative of one of their parishioners. *No time off for pastors or their families*, Diana thought. *Not even holidays.* Thankfully they'd been able to reach the teenage daughter of one of their congregants who agreed to keep Lizzie and Micah busy in the children's church room while Diana and Virginia and a couple of other ladies cooked and finished the last-minute preparations. More than once Diana had used the back of her hand to wipe sweat from her forehead. The weather was cool outside, with a slim chance of rain, but the church kitchen was at least ten degrees warmer than what Diana considered comfortable. Still, if Virginia, who was more than double Diana's age, could keep going without complaint, Diana was determined to do the same.

"It appears we're out of basil," Virginia announced, grabbing Diana's attention. "We're going to need that for the dressing."

Diana nodded, processing the older woman's nonverbal request. "I'm sure I have some at home," she said, untying her apron and hanging it near the kitchen door. "If not, I'll run to the store and get some."

She almost hoped she wouldn't have any so she'd have an excuse to escape the steamy kitchen for a little while, though she wasn't sure which stores, if any, might be open on Thanksgiving Day. But sure enough, she had plenty of basil.

She slipped it into her pocket and sighed as she headed back to the church. The cool air had felt good as she walked from the church to her home, but now she shivered as she hurried down the pathway to the church's back entrance. By the time she got back inside, she found herself welcoming the kitchen's warmth, not to mention the delicious smells of spices and fruit from the already cooling pies.

Dessert is done, she told herself. *Now to get the turkeys stuffed and into the ovens.* She knew it would take both of the kitchen's large ovens to accommodate the main course.

Virginia and the other ladies had all four turkeys washed and ready to go as soon as the stuffing was done. Diana shook her head as she watched Virginia tackle the next task with gusto. How a woman her age had managed to wrestle even one of those birds into submission, Diana couldn't imagine. *Experience, I guess*, she thought.

Since they now had the basil they needed, they should be able to have the turkeys stuffed and in the ovens in no time. Things looked to be progressing nicely. The next step would be to peel the potatoes and make sure the salads and cranberries were ready and in the fridge before starting on the vegetables.

Then it hit her. "Rolls," she said aloud. "We forgot to get the rolls. I'd better go see if I can find a store open so we can get some."

Virginia's flour-streaked face beamed at her. "No need, *mija*. I whipped some up yesterday—about six dozen of them. That should be enough, don't you think? They're over there, under the tea towels." She pointed toward the back corner of the long countertop.

Stunned, Diana stepped over to the tea towels and lifted one to peek underneath. Perfectly shaped and golden brown, the rolls nearly beckoned her to try one. Resisting the temptation, she placed the tea towel back over them and turned to Virginia.

"You're amazing," she said. "How in the world do you manage to do so much at . . . at . . . ?"

Virginia chuckled and her eyes twinkled. "At my age?"

Diana felt her face grow hot. Virginia was right. That was what she'd been about to say, though she marveled at Virginia's accomplishments at any age.

Virginia patted her arm. "It's all right, my dear. It's no secret that I'm not a spring chicken anymore. But I'm not dead yet, and so long as the good Lord leaves me here—despite the fact that He knows I'm anxious to go home—I assume He still has things for me to do. So I just get up in the morning and ask Him to help me do those things, whatever they are. Then off I go—although admittedly a bit more slowly than some years ago—and trust God to help me do what He's called me to do." She leaned a bit closer and lowered her voice a notch. "Of course, I no longer have little ones to keep me busy. It was much more difficult to get things done in those days. So believe me, I understand." She chuckled again and returned to the sink to chop the last of the vegetables for the stuffing.

Diana watched her in humbled wonder. *No wonder You say the older women in the church should teach the younger, Lord. I've been a pastor's wife for several years now, but being around Virginia makes me realize how much I still have to learn.* She smiled. *Thank You for putting her in my life, Father. I'll try to pay attention to what You want me to learn from her.*

"Mommy, can my new friend come to our house to play?"

Diana stopped with her fork midair and turned to her daughter, who sat beside her at the long, amply loaded table. Thirty-two people had shown up — mostly parishioners but also family and friends of parishioners, as well as a couple of people from the neighborhood who didn't normally attend church . . . and the homeless family. Diana knew who Lizzie referred to as her "new friend." Still, she had to ask.

She smiled at her daughter, dressed in her holiday best with her long brown hair pulled back in a ponytail and tied with a red ribbon to match her dress. Micah sat on Lizzie's other side, next to Paul. Micah too was dressed for the occasion, with what had been a clean white shirt less than an hour earlier. It was now spotted with cranberries and gravy, but Diana told herself she should have made him wear some sort of bib if she wanted to keep his clothes clean.

"So who's your new friend, sweetheart?" she asked, not allowing her gaze to flicker from Lizzie's face to the somewhat tattered-looking family of three who sat across and down a few places from them. She'd met them when they first came in, accompanied by Virginia's son, Albert, and his wife, Karen. Diana knew Virginia's son and daughter-in-law attended another church, but Virginia had explained to her that she thought it would be helpful for the family to come to Desert Sands's Thanksgiving dinner as a sort of outreach and welcome to them from the community.

Diana had welcomed them warmly, though the parents seemed to duck their heads and speak only when spoken to. The little girl, whom Diana figured wasn't much older than Lizzie, was a bit more outgoing.

Lizzie's brown eyes opened wide, as if surprised by her mother's question. She turned and pointed across the table toward the homeless family. "Right there," she said. "Sarah. She's five."

Diana's cheeks flamed as chatter stopped and nearly everyone looked their way. She smiled a general smile of acknowledgment and said, "Yes, honey. I met Sarah earlier. And we'll talk about her coming over to play with you later. For now we need to finish dinner so we can get to the desserts."

"I want punkin pie," Micah announced, lifting his hand into the air as if responding to a question in class. "With lots of whip cream."

Chuckles around the long table helped return the mood to what it had been before Lizzie's question. Diana sighed with relief, though she still wondered how best to explain to her daughter that Sarah and her parents might not be staying around too long. She had no idea what their arrangements were with Albert and Karen, or if they were making any progress at getting their car fixed or finding jobs and a place of their own. She certainly hoped so, and she promised herself she'd pray about the situation until it was resolved. But for right now, she didn't feel ready to discuss it with her daughter.

She glanced over her children's heads and quickly met Paul's eyes. They shone with understanding as he nodded, sending her the silent encouragement she needed. Why was it he seemed to know her so very well when it came to most everyday things, but when it involved one of the most difficult and disrupting events of their lives, he seemed clueless?

The problem of whether or not Lizzie's new friend could come home to play with her was easily resolved after dinner. With several more helpers in the kitchen, the cleanup went quickly. As Diana returned from the kitchen to recheck the long table in the fellowship hall — and even under the table where the children sat — she noticed her husband talking with the little girl and her parents. She wasn't surprised when he drew them into a tight circle and they joined hands as Paul prayed. She couldn't hear what was said, but she noticed the woman dabbing at her eyes with a tissue when they were done.

When Paul looked up and spotted Diana watching them, he motioned for her to join them. Although she was beat, she set down her wet sponge and towel then headed toward them, her smile genuine despite some unnamed misgivings.

"This is my wife, Diana," Paul announced as she stepped up next to him. "Honey, this is the McDonald family — Doug and Marie and their daughter, Sarah."

"I'm five," the little girl announced, her red braids lying smoothly down her back.

"So I've heard." Diana stuck out her hand, and the little girl took it, her grin widening in the process, showing a gap where her two top front teeth had been. "Hello again, Sarah." Diana looked back at Paul. "We all met briefly when they first arrived."

She then nodded at Doug and Marie. "I'm so glad you could join us here today. It was a delight having you — and I know our daughter, Lizzie, was especially pleased to meet Sarah."

"I've invited the McDonalds to stop by this weekend — Friday or Saturday, whichever day works out best for the ladies." Paul's smile flashed from Diana to Marie and back. "You girls just let us know, and Doug and I will be happy to oblige." Turning his gaze toward Doug, he lifted an eyebrow questioningly. "Right?"

The man, who looked only slightly younger than Paul, nodded. "Yeah, sure," he mumbled.

Paul shifted his gaze back to Diana. "I think Lizzie will be especially pleased."

Diana smiled and nodded. "Absolutely. She already asked me about having her 'new friend' over to play."

Sarah McDonald clasped her hands together and looked from one parent to the other. "Can we? Please? Please, please, puh-leeze?" She rolled her eyes for emphasis and began to bounce on her toes, no doubt doing additional damage to her already scruffy black tennis shoes. Diana's heart squeezed as she realized the child probably had no other shoes — unlike Lizzie, who had an abundance of clothes and shoes. Diana took in a deep breath and sighed. *We have so much, Lord—so many blessings! How dare I be ungrateful for anything?*

Before she could sink too deeply into self-condemnation, she turned to Sarah's mother and said, "Which is better for you, Marie? I'm flexible either way."

It was the first time Diana had seen the frail-looking woman smile, though it was hesitant. It did, however, make her more attractive—at least, in Diana's eyes.

"Would . . . would tomorrow be too soon?"

The woman's simple question tugged at Diana's heart. "Tomorrow would be perfect." She widened her smile. "And if you don't mind leftover turkey, why don't you all just come for dinner?"

Marie's dark eyes widened and she looked up at her husband, as if seeking his approval. Diana cast a quick glance at her own husband and saw that he was smiling and nodding at her.

"Sure," Doug said, his voice just a notch above a whisper. "I guess so."

Marie turned back to Diana. "That would be wonderful," she said. "What time, and what can I bring?"

Diana shrugged. "About five? That'll give the children time to play before dinner. And don't worry about bringing anything. We have plenty . . ."

Her voice trailed off as she caught the exchange between Doug and Marie. "Really," the woman said then. "I'd like to bring something."

Realizing her mistake in not accepting Marie's offer, she said, "Well . . . sure. If you really want to. What would you like to bring?"

Sarah, who was again bouncing up and down, tapped Diana on the arm. "My mama makes the best homemade chocolate cake ever," she announced. "And I mean, *ever!*"

The grown-ups chuckled, with even Doug entering in. "All right, then," Diana declared. "We'll see you around five. And don't forget to bring the best chocolate cake *ever*."

Mommy, I'm so excited that my new friend is coming over tomorrow."

Diana smiled down at her daughter, her hair splayed across the pillow and her pink cheeks matching her pajamas. Lizzie had repeated the phrase at least a dozen times since they came home from the Thanksgiving church dinner.

"I know you are," Diana said, gently brushing back a few stray strands from the girl's face then pulling the covers up to just beneath Lizzie's chin. "But for now you have to go to sleep. It's been a long and busy day, and we need to rest."

The child fixed her eyes on Diana. "Are you happy that my new friend and her family are coming?"

"Of course I am." She leaned down to kiss Lizzie's forehead. "Why would you ask?"

The girl shrugged. "I don't know. I think you looked at them funny."

Diana frowned. "Funny? What do you mean, Lizzie?" She could see an array of emotions dancing across her daughter's face, and she knew the girl was struggling with finding an answer.

"It was like . . . like you didn't want them there." She paused. "At the church, I mean."

Flames shot up Diana's neck to her cheeks, and she took a deep breath, wondering how to answer Lizzie's accusation, even if the girl hadn't meant it to sound like one.

"Sweetheart, I am so sorry if I looked that way to you, or to anyone else. I truly didn't mean to make the McDonalds feel unwelcome." Her heart pounded in her ears as she waited for her daughter's reply.

"I know that, Mommy. You're not mean. You're always nice to people. You just looked at them funny for a little while." She grinned. "Now my new friend is coming to see me tomorrow. I can't wait!"

Diana forced a smile and nodded. "Thank you, Lizzie. I'll remember that and ask God to help me *not* look at anyone funny ever again. I never want to make anyone feel unwelcome, especially at church."

Lizzie's arms popped up from underneath the covers, and she folded her hands in front of her face. "I'll pray too, Mommy. Can we do it now?"

A smattering of hot tears bit the back of Diana's eyelids. "Of course we can, baby." She closed her eyes and folded her hands as well. She wondered if she should start or let Lizzie do so. It didn't take long to find out the answer.

"Dear God," Lizzie began, "I'm so excited that my new friend is coming over to play tomorrow. But Mommy's kinda worried that she might've hurt my friend's feelings — and her parents' feelings, too. Please take away that funny look from Mommy so she won't do it ever again."

Diana was about to add her own brief request to her daughter's, but before she could, Lizzie said, "And thanks for bringing me a new friend. I'm so excited that she's coming over! Amen."

Diana blinked back her tears and leaned down to hug her daughter. "Thank you for that wonderful prayer, Lizzie. I love you."

"I love you too, Mommy," the girl replied, reaching her arms up and around her mother's neck. "But I only have one more question."

Surprised, Diana pulled back so she could look down at Lizzie's face. "And what would that be, sweetheart?"

"You said my friend's last name is McDonald. Are they the same ones in the song that had a farm? Because if they are, I *really* want to go see it!"

As realization dawned on Diana, she couldn't help but laugh. "No, honey. They're not the same people as the MacDonalds in the song. Now get some sleep. Today was a big day, and it looks like tomorrow is going to be another one."

She gave Lizzie one final kiss on the forehead and then stood and went to the door. She turned off the light and stepped out into the hallway, pulling the door only halfway shut. Smiling, she shook her head and went to the front room, where she knew she'd find Paul with his feet up, watching the tail end of a football game. She knew he'd get as big a kick out of their daughter's latest comment as she had.

The football game was over, but Paul's mind had drifted away, back to their life in Port Mason, particularly those last days as they prepared to move to Desert Sands. His adrenaline had kept him going at full tilt, rejoicing that God had granted his heart's desire to be a senior pastor at a church. It was something he'd dreamed of and prayed about for years, even before he met Diana. But as their relationship grew, she seemed to take on Paul's dream as her own. How many times over the years had they talked about that very thing, always seeming to be in agreement about its eventuality?

Then things changed. Or to be more accurate, Diana changed. He first noticed it the very day he told her about the offer. *I answered all her concerns, didn't I, Lord? I explained everything to her about where we would live and even what we would live on with such a small congregation. I thought surely she'd understand, especially when I told her that Dayspring was going to support us financially until the church grew large enough to pay us on their own. And then we*

have the money from the sale of our house, so it's not like we have no
savings. Seriously, Father, I'm so happy that You provided us with a
parsonage that we don't even have to pay for. It's perfect for our little
family, Lord—and for this community. It's such a missions field here,
and you're already starting to bring new people in. So why do I still
feel like my wife isn't with me on this? Should I be concerned about
our . . . relationship?

"Paul?"

Diana's voice penetrated his thoughts and prayers. For some reason he felt surprised when he lifted his eyes and saw her standing there in front of him. But she was smiling, and that warmed his heart.

"Hey," he said, "you and Lizzie must have had quite a mother-daughter talk. I kissed her goodnight and prayed with her after we'd gotten Micah tucked in, then I came in here and waited." He glanced at his watch and grinned. "Did you two solve all the world's problems?"

She sat down next to him on the couch and snuggled close. "Absolutely. At least, all the world's problems of a four-year old." She giggled. "Would you believe she thought the McDonalds might be the same MacDonalds in the song?"

Paul lifted his eyebrows questioningly then the light came on. "As in old MacDonald and his farm?"

Diana nodded. "The very same. I think she was a bit disappointed when I told her they weren't. She was hoping to go see their farm and all the animals."

Paul slid his arm around her shoulders and pulled her close. "I wonder if she even understands the family was living in their car until Albert and his wife took them in."

"I don't think so, but I didn't try to get into it. You know how she is if she gets too wound up. We'd *never* get her to sleep."

"True. You made the right decision." He sighed. "I'm glad the family's coming over tomorrow. I'd like to get to know them a little better. I wish I was better acquainted with people here in Desert Sands. I'd love to help them get jobs and a place of their own, but so far my range of influence, as sketchy as it may be, is pretty much limited to our small congregation and a few people here in our immediate neighborhood."

Diana lifted her head and kissed Paul's cheek. "I love that about you," she said. "You're always looking for ways to help people. And you accept them just the way they are, even though you want to encourage them to do better."

Paul shrugged. "I think that's in my job description."

She smiled up at him and nodded. "If it is — and it no doubt should be if it isn't—then you're doing a bang-up job, Pastor Michaelson."

She lowered her gaze and settled her head on his shoulder as they both turned their attention to the television. Paul knew Diana wasn't overly excited about football, but he appreciated that she often came and watched it with him. Now if he could just figure out how she could be so loving and considerate and yet still have problems adjusting to this new position in their lives.

The house was warm and cozy when the McDonalds arrived on their doorstep. Diana had lit several holiday-scented candles that now permeated the air, and Paul had started a fire in the fireplace in the front room. When the doorbell rang precisely at five, Diana looked up from the pot of turkey soup she was stirring. Should she answer the door? No, she decided. Paul was in the front room, tending the fire, so he'd no doubt go to greet them.

As it turned out, neither Paul nor Diana was the first one at the door. Lizzie nearly flew down the hallway and yanked the door open as she cried, "You're here! You're here!"

Diana chuckled as she opted to go meet everyone at the front door now that they'd been officially greeted. Sure enough, the two girls were already chattering away, holding hands as they skipped down the hallway toward Lizzie's bedroom.

"Look who's here, Mommy," Lizzie cried as they zipped past her, one brown ponytail and two red braids bouncing as they ran. They stopped at the bedroom door and Lizzie looked back at her mother. "Guess what? Sarah has red braids just like Pippi Longstocking!" Then, giggling, they disappeared into Lizzie's room.

Diana was still smiling as she joined the others in the entryway. Everyone seemed to be chuckling at Lizzie's last remark.

"It isn't the first time Sarah's been told that," Marie explained, "though most children their age don't even know who Pippi Longstocking is anymore."

Paul shook his head. "Oh, no, that wouldn't be us. I can't tell you how many times we've sat through Pippi Longstocking videos."

Diana reached out to Marie and pulled her into a quick hug. "Welcome," she said. "I'm so glad you could come."

"I am too," Marie answered, her green eyes shining just a bit. "It smells wonderful in here!"

"Turkey soup," Paul announced. "One of Diana's specialties."

Diana smiled. "You smell turkey soup *and* an assortment of scented candles."

"I hope you didn't make dessert," Marie said. "The chocolate cake is in the car."

"I wouldn't dream of trying to compete with the best chocolate cake *ever*," she said. "In fact, I've been nearly dreaming about it since yesterday."

As Paul and Doug, trailed closely by Micah, went out to the car to get the cake, Diana led Marie into the kitchen.

"How about a cup of coffee?" she asked as her guest sat down at the table. "Better yet, I was thinking about making some wassail. What do you think?"

This time there was no doubt that Marie's eyes were shining. "I haven't had wassail in years. My grandmother used to make that delicious hot cider for every holiday, but somehow we let the tradition fade away in our family."

As the woman sat down in one of the chairs around the table, Paul came in, carefully carrying the cake. He set it down on the counter while the women watched, Diana *oohing* and *aahing* over the chocolate creation.

Paul excused himself to rejoin Doug and Micah in the front room, and Diana transferred her attention to Marie. Her face had lost its brightness of a few moments ago, and she lowered her eyes momentarily before looking back up at Diana. A hint of tears shone in her eyes then, but Diana thought it best not to mention them.

"I know what you mean," Diana said, reaching down to the cupboard where she kept her large pots and pans. She pulled one out and set it on top of the stove before gathering the necessary ingredients. "I always thought I'd keep my family's holiday traditions going, but I'm afraid most of them have gotten lost over the years. My mom and stepdad live in New Jersey and take turns spending the holidays with me and my two brothers and their families. We got them last year, so it'll be a couple more years before they come here again." She shrugged. "And who knows where we'll be living by then, right? Circumstances can change so quickly. Why, just this time last year, when my parents were getting ready to join us for Christmas, we were living in the most lovely home in — "

Her voice trailed off at the somewhat stricken expression of her guest, jolting Diana into the reality of what she'd just said. Her cheeks flamed and she hurried to sit down next to Marie. Taking the woman's hand in her own, she breathed a silent prayer for help.

"I am *so* sorry, Marie. Truly, I wasn't thinking. That must have sounded so selfish of me, talking about the beautiful home we used to have, when here we are, comfortable and warm in the parsonage God's provided for us. Please forgive me."

Marie's tears were shining again, but she squeezed Diana's hands. "You have nothing to apologize for. I'm so grateful to you for having us over today. When I got sick and then Doug got laid off and we lost our health insurance . . ." She took a deep breath before continuing. "It seemed like everything hit at once. We lost our home, our furniture, everything besides one car and what we could fit in it. We wore out our welcome with all our relatives, none of whom had the extra cash it would take to get us back into a place of our own. Even a tiny rented apartment is more than we can afford on the little bit of unemployment Doug gets." She blinked, no doubt trying to rid herself of her tears.

"We were passing through Desert Sands on our way to Ventura. Doug has a friend there who thought he could get Doug a job where he works, but then our car broke down. We managed to push it to the side of the road, but that was about it. We had no extra money for car repairs." She shook her head, no longer trying to stop the tears that trickled down her face. "We thought things couldn't get much worse. We couldn't even get Sarah registered in school because we weren't sure where we'd end up."

Diana continued to pray silently and to hold Marie's hand as the woman shared her story.

"That's when we met Albert at the grocery store. We were picking up a few things to eat when Sarah accidentally knocked over a display. Albert was loading his own grocery basket just behind us when it happened. He went right over and helped Doug restack everything, introducing himself in the process. We thanked him and then saw him again when we were checking out." Her face reddened. "I know he saw how carefully Doug was counting out his money to pay for our groceries. Then Albert followed us out into the parking lot. I guess when he realized we didn't have a car, he decided to offer us a ride."

Marie swallowed and took a couple of deep breaths. "I can't tell you how badly I wanted to accept, but how could we? The last thing we wanted was for someone to realize we were homeless. We'd been sleeping in our car since it broke down a couple days earlier, but we knew it was just a matter of time before someone reported us." She began to sob. "My greatest fear is that the authorities would take Sarah away from us. I've learned to give up everything else we've lost, but I could never go on if we lost our little girl."

Diana's heart twisted inside her as she thought of how she'd feel if she lost either of her own children, whatever the circumstances. True, she'd sat at a mother's side more than once, trying to offer comfort and prayers to someone who had just lost a child. But, this was one of the first times she'd done it since having her own children — it wasn't until this moment that she'd realized how truly devastating such a loss could be.

She put her arms around her guest and let her cry. After a few moments Marie pulled back and looked into Diana's eyes. "Albert was a godsend that day — literally. It's been years since I've been in church, and Doug has never attended, but ever since we met Albert and he offered to help, I've been praying again. Albert and Karen took us into their own home, loaned us the money to fix our car, and are even helping Doug look for a job." She shook her head. "I don't know what would've happened to us if Albert hadn't come into our lives that day."

Marie offered a half-smile. "When he invited us to go to the Thanksgiving dinner at your church yesterday, I was really scared. I mean, I couldn't imagine what nice church people like you and Pastor

Paul would think of us. But you were all so welcoming, so . . ." She shook her head again. "So wonderful. Thank you again for inviting us into your beautiful home."

This time it was Diana who let the tears trickle from her eyes and down her cheeks as she pulled Marie into another embrace. "We're so glad you came, Marie. You are a blessing to us . . . truly."

It was a great day, wasn't it?" Paul asked as he returned from the hallway bathroom to the bedroom, wearing blue-striped pajamas and fuzzy brown slippers.

They'd put the kids to bed earlier—all three of them, since the girls had convinced both sets of parents to let Sarah spend the night. Micah had seemed perturbed over Lizzie having a friend over when he didn't, but Paul had made an extra effort to include him in the "man stuff" Paul and Doug did. When Paul had offered to take Micah to ride go-carts, modified for younger children, at a nearby amusement park on Saturday, Micah was ecstatic and went to bed without argument.

"A really great day," Diana agreed. "Not to mention the best chocolate cake *ever*." She kept her eyes on Paul as he grinned at her remark then turned off the light and climbed into bed.

"You have to admit," he said, fluffing his pillow, "it was really, really good."

"So good I noticed you had a second piece."

He pulled her close, and she laid her head on his shoulder. "And you didn't?"

"I tried not to," she admitted, "but I couldn't resist."

Paul chuckled. "I'm just glad you insisted they take a big chunk of it home. It's bad enough that nearly a quarter of that best-ever chocolate cake is still sitting in our kitchen . . . calling my name."

"You don't have to answer."

"Yeah, right. Just like you could have resisted that second piece."

She sighed. "You got me."

They lay quietly for a few moments then Paul commented, "You and Marie seemed to get along well."

"We did. Before dinner she told me a little about how they ended up homeless. It broke my heart, especially when I realized how easily something like that could happen."

"True. And poor Doug, he just wants to work and take care of his family. He's not a believer, but he's a really nice family man who wants to do the right thing." He paused. "Did Marie tell you she might have cancer? She might not, of course, but they can't afford to have the tests done until they get some insurance. Albert's trying to help them get it from the state now."

Diana rose up on her elbow and peered down at Paul in the semi-darkness. "Cancer?" She sighed. "No, she didn't tell me that part. She said she'd been sick, and I noticed she looks a bit frail, but . . ." She shook her head. "Now it's even worse. What are we going to do?"

"*We?* So you're onboard to help them, I see."

Diana felt her cheeks flush, though she knew Paul couldn't see them. "You know what I mean. Sweetheart, we have to do something. But what? She said Albert and Karen are helping them look for a job and letting them stay at their house. They even loaned them the money to get their car fixed. But there must be something we can do — especially about Marie's health."

Paul drew her back down to his chest. "How about if we start with praying for them? Regularly, you and me, every day. And I invited Doug to come to church on Sunday. He said he'd think about it. Apparently he hasn't got much experience with the Bible."

"According to Marie, none at all. She hinted that she might have had some as a child, but she admitted it's been ages since she's been in a church. But I think they really liked the church dinner yesterday, don't you?"

Paul nodded, his head resting on top of Diana's. "I do, yes. And I believe God has brought them here for a reason — several reasons, no doubt — so let's make ourselves available any way God wants us to help make that happen."

Diana sighed, feeling more relaxed than she had in quite some time. "Yes, let's do that," she murmured, as she felt herself drifting off to the steady beat of her husband's heart.

Diana found herself envying Paul. He was out with Micah riding a go-cart, but at least he had only one child with him. She'd been overseeing both girls for several hours now. She'd thought she could get them to do something quiet in Lizzie's room, but each time she'd steer them in a specific direction, they'd come bouncing out of the room a few minutes later, wanting a snack or to watch TV or to "help" her in the kitchen. She'd fielded each request as it came in, but she was quickly running out of options.

Who'd think two little girls could create so much noise? She smiled at the question. Had she forgotten what she was like when she was little? Her mom always called her a chatterbox, but now the word had come to life.

She sighed. "All right, Diana. Just do it. Go in there and ask them if they'd like to help you make cookies."

"Who are you talking to, Mommy?"

Diana turned to find two sets of wide eyes — one brown, one green — staring up at her from the kitchen entryway. She hadn't heard them coming, but there they were, adorable and anxiously awaiting her answer.

She smiled. "I'm afraid I was just thinking out loud."

"But you said *cookies*, Mommy. I heard you."

Sarah nodded. "I heard you, too."

Well, she had no choice now. Making cookies it was.

"You're right about that part. I was thinking that the three of us could make cookies together. What do you — ?"

"Yay!"

"Cookies!"

"Chocolate chip! I want chocolate chip!"

The girls jumped around, alternately grabbing one another and jumping in tandem, then letting go and jumping alone. But with each jump they cried out another word of excitement.

Seemed she'd touched on a good idea. So why did she still feel so hesitant? It wasn't like she'd never let Lizzie "help" with simple cooking, including shaking sprinkles on freshly baked sugar cookies. But now there were two little girls to supervise — and try to tone down a bit. No small assignment.

"All right," she called over their happy exclamations. "We can't make cookies while we're jumping up and down and hollering. We need to settle down and put on aprons so we don't mess up our clothes."

As the girls quieted, Diana reached inside the pantry and pulled three aprons off the hook. Hers was a simple matter of slipping it over her head and tying it behind her back, but getting them on the girls was another story.

After a couple of failed attempts and lots of giggles and squeals of delight, they managed to fold the aprons enough so they wouldn't drag on the floor when the girls walked. The next thing was to set them up at the table where they could kneel on chairs and be tall enough to take turns stirring batter. It took twice as long as usual for Diana to supervise the girls as they put ingredients into the large mixing bowl on the table between them, but at last they were ready to start mixing the dough.

"It looks delicious, Mommy. Can I eat some?"

Diana shook her head. "Not yet. There are raw eggs in there, so we're going to wait until the cookies are baked. But you two can have the first ones. The bakers get that privilege."

The girls exchanged a conspiratorial look, obviously pleased at being the ones with the special privilege of testing the cookies before anyone else.

Sarah lifted her slightly freckled face, her red braids spilling down her back. "Mommy let me help stir the chocolate cake yesterday, just like we're stirring now. But I didn't get the first piece because we were bringing it here to you."

"Ah yes, the best chocolate cake *ever*. And it was! But now we have to focus on cookies, right?"

The girls nodded, and Sarah spoke again. "It was fun helping Mommy make the cake yesterday. It was the first time we made a cake in a long time because we didn't have a kitchen."

Diana's heart squeezed at the reminder of the McDonalds' circumstances. But there was something else, something that had nagged her more and more lately, leaving her unsettled and even somewhat fearful. Instead of letting herself wonder what it might be, she dismissed it as she always did. Then she prayed silently that God would provide the McDonalds with a job and a place to live — and the insurance they needed to find out about Marie's health situation.

She shook her head as she watched the girls taking turns stirring the batter — with surprisingly little contention over whose turn it was — and she asked God to forgive her for the petty things she allowed to captivate her thoughts and feelings. At least her husband had a job, and she and her family had a place to live. How could she complain about her own situation when she had it better than so many others?

Thank You, Lord. And please help me to focus on being grateful.

"Mommy, it was *sooo* much fun! Daddy rode with me, but he let me drive!"

Diana glanced above Micah's head and saw Paul give her a wink. She smiled as she looked down at her son. "That sounds like a really fun adventure."

Micah nodded, his blue eyes dancing. "Yep. It was. And Daddy said I did so good we can go again tomorrow."

Diana lifted her eyebrows in surprise just as Paul laid a hand on Micah's shoulder. "Whoa! Hold on a minute there, buddy. I said we could do it again *soon*, not tomorrow."

Micah's smile faded. "But tomorrow is soon."

Diana saw her husband swallow a laugh. "Yes, it is. You're right. But I didn't mean *that* soon. Maybe in a few weeks, OK?"

Micah's shoulders slumped. "A few weeks? That's a really long time."

"It'll go by before you know it," Paul said. "And besides, we need to get ready for Christmas. That'll be here *really* soon."

Micah's eyes went wide again. "How many days?"

"Thirty," Paul said.

"Thirty! That's almost a million!" A frown appeared on Micah's forehead. "It'll *never* get here."

"Tell you what," Diana said, bending down to speak directly to her son. "You know my big calendar here in the kitchen?"

Micah nodded, though his expression was wary.

"Let's go look at it right now. We'll make a big X over today, and then every morning we'll make another X for the day. We'll also put a circle around Christmas day so you can see how close we're getting. What do you think?"

"Will Christmas come faster that way?"

Paul and Diana laughed aloud. Micah seemed puzzled, but continued looking at his mother as he awaited her answer.

"Not really," she said, "but it will make it *seem* faster."

Micah grinned. "OK. Let's put a X on today."

Paul ruffled Micah's blond curls. "OK, buddy, you and Mommy can take care of the calendar." He directed his next statement to Diana. "I need to track down a couple of phone numbers that I don't have here, so I'll be over at my office for a few minutes."

Diana nodded as she escorted her son to the wall by the sink, where the calendar hung at eye-level for her. She lifted him up so he could sit on the counter, then she pointed at today's date. "This is today," she explained. She grabbed the pen that hung on a string beside the calendar. "Can you make an X on that spot?"

"Yep." Micah took the pen, his tongue between his teeth as he concentrated, then drew a relatively straight X on the day's date. He looked at Diana. "Can we do tomorrow too, so Christmas can come faster?"

Diana chuckled and shook her head. "No, I'm afraid we can't make Christmas come any faster by drawing more X's. One a day. That's all." She lifted the November page to reveal December below it, then pointed toward the 25th. "When we get this far, it'll be Christmas. Do you want to make a circle around that day?"

Micah nodded and drew a fairly round O around the 25th. "Now what?" he asked, letting go of the pen and fixing his eyes on Diana.

She smiled. "Well, since I know you and Daddy ate lunch out and it's still several hours until dinner, how would you like to try one of the cookies your sister and Sarah made this morning?"

"Only one?" he asked. "Can I have two?"

Diana chuckled, reminding herself to have Micah help her the next time she made cookies. And who knew? Maybe Lizzie would enjoy going go-carting with her dad. She resolved to suggest it the next time Paul had some free time.

CHAPTER 18

It was Tuesday morning, and Diana was determined to make at least a minimal effort at nailing down the preliminaries for Paul's 40th birthday party the weekend before Christmas. She knew it wasn't a good time, since everyone was busy with pre-holiday activities on top of normally busy routines, but she really wanted to do this for Paul. *After all, turning 40 is a big deal — at least, it will be for me, even though I have a few years yet.*

She glanced at the children while she rinsed bowls and cups and spoons from breakfast and put them in the dishwasher. They seemed engrossed in the project she'd given them — a decorated Christmas tree coloring sheet with a large empty box under the tree. She told them to draw whatever they thought would be the perfect Christmas gift, and Lizzie had started in immediately. Micah, on the other hand, had seemed puzzled before he at last began drawing and coloring.

If all went well she could get her to-do and to-buy lists done before Paul came home for lunch. Once he was gone again, she'd put the children down for their naps. It was then that she'd call and personally invite a handful of close friends to a surprise party.

Who would comprise that "handful" of close friends was the difficulty she wrestled with now. If they were still in Port Mason, it would be easy. They had several couples they did everything with, so of course they'd be invited. But now they were in Desert Sands, and she supposed Paul would expect her to include people from their new church community. But did that mean she couldn't also invite friends from Port Mason? She knew she risked exceeding her self-imposed limit of a "handful" of close acquaintances, but she couldn't imagine omitting longtime friends.

She sighed. *I'd better get busy with those lists while the kids are still relatively quiet and before Paul comes in wanting lunch.* She snagged a pen and a pad of paper from the counter beside the phone then sat down at the table with Lizzie and Micah.

"Are you doing homework, too, Mommy?"

Micah's voice diverted her attention from her grocery list for the party. Yet even as she refocused on her children, the question over what snacks and appetizers to serve still tugged at the back of her mind.

"In a way, yes." She smiled at Micah then Lizzie, both of whom had stopped coloring to watch her. Then, wanting to head off any further questions about what she was doing and why, she asked, "So how are you two coming? You've both been working hard on your projects."

Nearly simultaneously, the children grabbed their paper and held it up for her to see. Both pictures were colorful, Micah's especially.

"Very nice," she said. "You're both using beautiful colors."

"But I don't color out of the lines like Micah," Lizzie announced. "That's 'cause I'm older."

Micah's retort was quick and loud. "I don't color out of the lines!"

"You do too. Look, Mommy! He colors out of the lines, right?"

Diana mentally replaced her party-planner hat with her counselor/teacher hat. "I think both your pictures are excellent. Lizzie, you truly are becoming a wonderful artist. And Micah, you're doing a great job, too — very colorful and cheerful. But now that you're almost done coloring, you need to decide what you want to put in the empty box. Any ideas yet?"

"I'm going to draw a puppy," Micah declared. "That's what I *really* want for Christmas."

Diana sighed. Micah had been asking for a dog for months now, but she kept hoping he'd forget about it and move on to something else.

"And what about you?" she asked Lizzie. "Have you thought about what you'd like to put in your Christmas box?"

She nodded. "A baby."

Diana felt her eyes widen. Was her daughter asking for a sister or another brother?

"I see," she said. "And what will you name the baby?"

Lizzie rolled her eyes. "You know, Mommy. Baby? Christmas?" She sighed. "His name is Jesus, remember?"

Diana smiled. "Yes, sweetheart, I remember. I should have realized that."

Appearing pleased to have cleared up her mother's confusion, Lizzie went back to her project, with Micah following her lead.

Now, back to her food list then on to her decoration list. She'd keep it all as simple as possible, especially because she was going to have to figure out a way to get the decorations up and the food ready without Paul noticing. She wished she still lived a few blocks from the Kelloggs in Port Mason. Having Megan onboard would help simplify everything. Not only was she an expert at putting together a party, surprise or otherwise, but she'd certainly offer her kitchen for cooking and decorating.

But I don't live near Megan anymore, so who am I going to get to help? The thought of Virginia popped into her mind, but she couldn't ask the elderly lady to get involved. It was far too much work for someone her age.

Then again . . . maybe she could at least hide the decorations and food ingredients at Virginia's home until the party. Now if she could just figure out how to keep Paul away that Saturday . . .

Her eyes fixed themselves on Micah's bowed head. He seemed completely engrossed in his drawing, but Diana's thoughts had bypassed the children's artwork and gone straight to Paul and Micah's go-cart outing. That would be perfect! She knew she'd get no argument from either of them; the only concern would be if the weather didn't cooperate. OK, so she'd have to come up with a plan B if A got washed out in rain. But at least she now had a starting place.

Pleased with herself, Diana returned to her lists with a renewed determination to make Paul's birthday the best ever.

Mitchell Green was pleased that Paul had made room for him in his weekly schedule. Of course, he'd had to agree to be a bit flexible when other priorities invaded Paul's week, but that hadn't happened often. Obviously Paul was as dedicated to their prayer time as he was.

Wednesday morning had dawned cool and crisp, the type of day Mitchell had preferred in his younger days. Now it seemed to aggravate his arthritis, though not as much as one of their occasional rainy days.

Brisk or not, Mitchell had opted to walk the few blocks from his home to the church. By the time the old building came into view, he was looking forward to the hot coffee he knew Paul would offer him.

He stepped through the unlocked door into the unheated sanctuary and came face to face with Pastor Paul and Byron Phillips. Both seemed in a hurry.

"Mitchell!" Paul stopped so quickly that Byron almost ran into him. "I'm afraid I won't be able to make our prayertime today." He hesitated as he cast a questioning look at Byron.

"It's all right, Pastor," Byron said. "Mitchell and I have known each other for years, and I know he's one of the greatest prayer warriors around." He offered his hand to Mitchell, who took it then pulled

Byron into a quick embrace. "I got a call from Max this morning. He's in . . . jail, you know."

Mitchell nodded. "I do know, yes. I've been praying for him — and for you."

Byron turned to Paul. "Can we bring Mitchell along? I can't imagine anyone I'd rather have praying for us right now."

Paul glanced at Mitchell, who nodded. "OK. We'll fill you in on the way, but basically Max called his dad and asked him to bring me to visit him today because he wants to pray and — as he put it — 'get things right with the Lord.'"

Mitchell's heart soared. He and Paul might not be having their weekly prayer meeting today as planned, but he was thrilled to be part of this "rescue mission." He started praying before they even made it to the car.

As previously approved clergy, Paul was able to accompany Byron as he went inside the jail for a visit with his son. Mitchell had opted to wait in the car and had assured them of constant prayer cover throughout their time with Max.

They didn't have long to wait. Within 15 minutes after they were cleared, Paul and Byron were called to the visiting room where they sat down on one side of a see-through glass partition. Max was already there, waiting on the other side, with the phone receiver pressed to his ear.

Byron looked at Paul, who nodded toward the receiver on their side of the partition. Byron returned the nod and picked it up.

"Hello, son." Byron's voice cracked, and he cleared his throat before trying again. "We got here as soon as we could."

Max nodded and mouthed words Paul couldn't hear.

Byron turned to Paul. "Max thanks us both for coming."

Paul nodded in Max's direction, continuing to pray silently, knowing that Mitchell was backing him up the entire time.

Max spoke again, a bit longer this time, then Byron handed the phone to Paul.

"He wants to talk to you."

Paul took the receiver and fixed his gaze on the young man with the dark eyes, seated on the opposite side of the partition. Max appeared nervous as he waited.

"Hello, Max," Paul said. "I'm glad you invited me to come along with your father. I'm . . . sorry I didn't come sooner, but I was under the impression you didn't want to see me."

"You were right," Max replied. "I didn't want to see anyone before, but — " He shook his head. "But now I know I need to talk to you, even though we've never met. Still, I woke up thinking about you in the middle of the night, so I asked for permission to make a call as soon as possible. Thanks for getting here so fast."

Paul nodded again. "So . . . how can I help you, Max? Your dad said you wanted us to pray with you and to help you make things right with the Lord. Is that true?"

Max swallowed, his Adam's apple bobbing up then down. Then he took a deep breath. "Yes. It's true. My parents raised me in the church, and I used to pray and read my Bible when I was little. But somehow, somewhere, I gave all that up." His shoulders slumped. "And look where it got me."

Paul's heart ached for the young man. "It's never too late to turn to God, Max. You know that."

Max nodded. "I know. That's why I called my dad. I don't want it to be too late for me — even in here."

Paul smiled. "It doesn't matter where you are. You're never alone. God is on your side of this partition just as surely as He's on this side."

The hint of a smile played across Max's face. "So what do I do? How do I make things right? I've been trying to pray by myself, but I feel like God's not listening. I thought about asking for the chaplain, but then I decided I'd rather have my dad's pastor come instead."

"I'm sure the chaplain is a good man and would help you in any way you need it, but I'm honored that you asked for me." He breathed a silent prayer then plunged ahead.

"Max, if you were raised in the church and had praying, Bible-reading parents — which I know you did — then you know the basic Scriptures about salvation. Am I right?"

"I remember John 3:16: 'For God so loved the world that He gave His only begotten Son, that whoever believes in Him should not perish but have everlasting life.'"

"Perfect. You didn't miss a word."

"I remember a few others," Max offered, "but that one most of all. I've been thinking about it a lot lately, mainly because it's one of the first ones I learned when I was a kid. But . . ." He paused. "I thought I believed in Him then, but I haven't been to church or prayed in years. I even invited Jesus into my heart in my third-grade Sunday School class, and then I got baptized. But like I said . . ."

"You're wondering if you lost the relationship you had with God when you were little, and if you've wandered too far to be able to come back."

Even through the partition, Paul could see the dampness reflected in Max's eyes. "You don't know what . . . what I've done, Pastor."

Tears stung Paul's eyes. How many times had he heard this lament from those who thought they were too far gone to ever make it back? More than he could count. "None of that matters, Max, not with God. Sure, there are always consequences for our behavior, and you'll most likely have to pay some sort of legal price for those things you've done, but that's not the case with God. When you come to

Him with an honest, repentant heart, He'll forgive you and restore you to relationship with Him. First John 1:9 says, 'If we confess our sins, He is faithful and just to forgive us our sins and to cleanse us from all unrighteousness.' Is that what you want to do now, Max?"

One of the tears glistening in Max's eyes slipped out and began to trickle down his face. He nodded, clearly struggling to maintain his composure. "Yes. I . . . I do."

"Then close your eyes and repeat after me as we pray. All right?"

Max nodded again and closed his eyes. A quick sideways glance told Paul that Byron had closed his as well.

Speaking in short phrases so Max could repeat them, Paul closed his eyes and began. "Father God, I thank You . . . that I never stopped being Your child . . . even when I strayed so far away . . . I confess that I have sinned, Lord . . . many times and in terrible ways . . . but Father, You said that if I would confess my sins to You . . . that You would forgive me and cleanse me . . . I'm doing that now, Father . . . confessing my sins and turning the rest of my life over to You . . . From this time forward I want to live for You . . . to walk close to You and to study Your Word and pray . . . and to tell others about what a wonderful God I now serve."

Max choked up on the last phrase and had to wipe away his tears before he could go on, but at last Paul and Max and Byron closed their prayer with a sturdy amen, knowing God had heard and answered. As they opened their eyes, Paul couldn't help but notice the softened look of peace and joy on Max's face.

"Remember, Max," Paul said, wishing he could reach through the partition and take the young man's hand in his own, "life won't suddenly get easy now that you're walking with God, but I promise you He'll walk with you every step of the way, even carrying you when you're not able to stand on your own." He smiled. "And now you need to request a visit from that chaplain. He'll know how to get you plugged in to Bible studies and church services here at the facility, and he'll be happy to help disciple you as you read your Bible and pray. I don't personally know the chaplain here, but I've heard really good things about him. Will you promise to do that at your very first opportunity, Max?"

"Today," Max answered, still wiping at his tears. "Right away."

Paul nodded. "Good. Then I'm going to leave now and let you and your dad have some time together." He looked at Byron, whose face shone. "I'll be waiting in the car with Mitchell."

CHAPTER 19

Paul spent much of the rest of that day preparing for his Wednesday evening teaching. He'd been working his way through the Book of Ephesians, leaving off the previous Wednesday at chapter 5 verse 22, a verse that generally stirred up a lot of emotions, particularly among married couples.

As he sat in his office that afternoon, reviewing his notes and praying, he couldn't help but notice that verse 21 laid the perfect groundwork for the section he'd be discussing that evening. He'd known that for quite some time, of course, but the verse seemed to call out to him on this sunny, cool Wednesday. He read it aloud: ". . . submitting to one another in the fear of God."

Paul pondered it for a moment then whispered, "What is it, Lord? Is there something different I should see in these otherwise familiar words?" He heard no voice but sat still, his eyes closed, as he let the words continue to wash over him until he began to get some clarity on what God was speaking to his heart.

At last he began to verbalize his thoughts. "Father, I see the obvious — that by continually 'submitting to one another in the fear of God' we will become humble enough to be able to practice this next section about husbands and wives in the way You intended. But is there something else? Something I've missed?"

The only response was the image of Diana coming into focus in his mind, and he smiled at the implications. "You have certainly given me the best wife a man could ever wish for, Lord. Thank You. And yes, I know I need to follow the teaching for husbands in this section to love my wife in the same way Your Son loved the church and gave Himself up for it. Show me, Father, if I've failed to do that somehow. Help me to walk in Your footsteps, Lord."

He continued to meditate on the words in verses 22–33, the section that would be his focus for the evening's teaching. He planned to open with the call of God for wives to willingly and joyfully submit to their husbands and for husbands to love their wives sacrificially. He would also focus on the final verse, which would tie the entire teaching together: "Nevertheless let each one of you in particular so love his own wife as himself, and let the wife *see* that she respects *her* husband." Not only did the verse strengthen God's call for men to love their wives unconditionally and self-sacrificially, but it also called for wives to *respect* their husbands. This verse — in fact, this entire section of Scripture — called for unconditional and sacrificial obedience, as Paul knew that not all husbands behaved in such a way as to earn their wife's respect. But, of course, God hadn't instructed wives to respect only the husbands who deserved it, but rather the husband He gave them. And that, he was certain, was an impossible calling in far too many circumstances — at least, if wives depended on their own fragile and limited strength to obey God's command. For God's will and purposes to be carried out in a marriage, husbands must depend on God's strength to love their wives unconditionally, and wives must do the same to show respect to their husbands.

Feeling as if he'd tied together his final thoughts and notes, he closed with a prayer then exited his office and went home to spend a little time with his family before that night's service.

Diana noticed there were a few more people in attendance that evening. Two of them she recognized from the Sunday morning crowd, and she was always pleased to see members of that group branching out to attend other services and functions. The other three were the McDonalds, and she was thrilled, as she knew Paul would be when he saw them. To date, except for the Thanksgiving dinner, they hadn't been back to the church, though Diana had hoped to see them on Sunday morning.

But they're here today, Lord, she thought. *Thank You!*

She had already dropped off Lizzie and Micah in the children's church room downstairs. Thankfully, Diana had found a few volunteers to help her teach the class. So, she was able to come to "big church" tonight. She wondered if Doug and Marie were unaware of the class, as Diana was certain Sarah would much prefer joining the other children than sitting up here with her parents.

She headed in their direction. "So glad to see you here," she said with a smile, reaching out to embrace Marie. "Did you know there's a class downstairs for kids? I'd be happy to show you where it is. Lizzie and Micah are already there."

Sarah's eyes lit up and she clasped her hands together as she looked from one parent to the other and back again, much as she'd done when Diana had invited the family for dinner the previous week.

"Oh, please, please, puh-leeze," she begged. "Can I please go down to the children's class with my friends? Please?"

Diana saw Doug and Marie exchange glances and smile. Marie looked down at Sarah. "All right," she said. "I don't see why not." She returned her gaze to Diana. "Sure, thanks. Let's go."

Diana led the way, with Marie and Sarah following. Doug had apparently opted to wait in the pew, which was fine with Diana. It gave her a few free moments with Marie.

"I'm so pleased to see you here," she said after they signed Sarah in. The moment she'd spotted Lizzie, Sarah had raced to her side. The girls were hugging and squealing with delight when Diana and Marie left to return to the sanctuary.

"And I'm happy to be here," Marie said. "I wanted to come on Sunday, but Doug was still a bit hesitant. Then, out of the blue, he suggested we come tonight. Can you believe it?"

Diana smiled. "I can. When God's up to something, anything can happen." She watched Marie's face to see how she would react to the statement.

Marie's smile was hesitant. "I sort of wondered the same thing." She leaned closer to Diana as they walked down the corridor toward the stairs. "Do you really think God is doing something in our lives?"

"Absolutely! He loves you very much, Marie. And Doug and Sarah, too."

Tears shone from Marie's eyes as they reached the stairway. "Thank you," she said, laying her hand on Diana's arm. "I'm so glad to have a friend like you."

Diana swallowed and blinked back her own tears. She tried to speak but just nodded and started up the stairs.

Diana felt her shoulders tighten when Paul announced his teaching for the night. He'd been doing a series on relationships, so she should have expected Ephesians 5 to pop up sooner or later. Husband-and-wife relationships were, after all, one of the most important human relationships on earth. And it wasn't like they'd never discussed the topic between themselves or heard others teach on it. So why was she having this strange reaction?

Forgive me, Lord, she prayed silently, *and please help me receive whatever your purpose is in this teaching tonight.*

Her shoulders relaxed only slightly as she waited for Paul to begin. He did so by reading verses 22–33, but then he went back and stressed the importance of the admonition in verse 21, "submitting to one another in the fear of God."

Paul looked out over the small congregation before he went on. "I thought it important to stress verse 21 in light of the following verses on husband-and-wife relationships. Though God has purposed a specific order in the way husbands and wives relate to one another, He has also called us to walk humbly in *all* areas of our lives. So if you're a husband who reads this passage of Scripture and feels tempted to remind your wife of her calling to submit to you, remember first the words in verse 21 about *all* of us submitting to one another. Keeping that reminder in place helps us walk out the rest of the passage in humility."

Paul then proceeded to work through the admonition to wives to submit to their husbands but also stressing the husband's responsibility to love his wife as Christ loved the church — sacrificially. Diana's shoulders were nearly back to normal when Paul wrapped up the teaching by repeating the verse he'd stressed at the beginning: "submitting to one another in the fear of God."

"This is so important," Paul said again. "None of us as men has the right to pound our chests and demand that our wives obey our commands. We are to love our wives unconditionally and selflessly, and that means in all areas of our marriage and life together." He leaned forward on the podium. "Men, that means something as simple as seeking your wife's input on decisions, however important or trivial those decisions may seem. If God has given us a godly wife . . ." He paused and flashed a smile at Diana. ". . . then He has provided us with a wise partner, one whose thoughts and feelings — and yes, her advice — should be taken into account before we make a final decision." He stood up straight again. "Trust me, fellas, it will go a long way in making for a happy home."

A couple of scattered chuckles followed his last remark before he asked the congregation to stand so they could pray together. Diana did so, but not without realizing that the tightness in her shoulders had returned.

CHAPTER 20

December had arrived, and Christmas shopping was in full swing, even in the small town of Desert Sands. With only one limited shopping center, many Desert Sands residents opted to drive to one of the nearby cities with more to offer.

Diana was no exception, and she so appreciated Paul for realizing that. He had even offered to take care of Lizzie and Micah so she could go shopping on her own. Thrilled, Diana had gladly accepted and had quickly made early lunch plans with Megan to meet at their favorite spot with a view of the ocean. Then they'd head to the bustling mall nearby and do some serious shopping.

As she'd been doing sporadically since that Wednesday night service, she recognized the vague unease that tried to pop into her mind again, then pushed it away and concentrated on the scenery as she drew nearer to Port Mason. Though the weather was cool and breezy, the sun shone overhead. Diana called ahead to the restaurant to be sure they could get a table with a view of the ocean.

She recognized the feeling of homesickness that grew stronger as she neared the place she so loved. Would she ever feel this way about Desert Sands?

The sign for the first Port Mason turnoff appeared on her right. She normally took the third exit, as it was the most direct route to her former home. But today she took that first exit in order to drive through downtown to see the Christmas decorations before heading to the restaurant. The decorations always stoked her excitement about the upcoming holidays.

I sure hope it works that way this year. So far my Christmas joy seems to be packed away in the ornament box in the attic. She reminded herself then that she'd better ask Paul to retrieve those decorations so they could get the tree up and decorated. *I should have had that done by now,* she thought as she exited the freeway. *No more procrastinating!*

Sure enough, the downtown shops and even the trees that lined the main streets were covered with red and green decorations. She smiled when she spotted a bell-ringer in front of the old hardware store. When she came to a stop sign, she lowered her window. The chill air was filled with the faint sound of carols coming from the park a couple of blocks away.

I forgot that several church choirs come at various times and sing carols in the square by the big tree. I imagine they had their lighting ceremony last weekend. Her heart squeezed at the memories of attending those ceremonies with Paul and the children, even as she marveled that no one had yet complained about the Christmas songs and decorations that had been banned in a few other places across the country.

She pulled into the lot by the park and turned off her engine. Since she had a few moments to spare, she decided to listen to the beautiful singing.

She closed her eyes and leaned her head against the headrest, letting the words permeate her heart as she prayed silently for God to help her get past whatever was holding her back from the feeling of joy that she so missed.

The promised seat by the window was waiting for them when Diana and Megan entered the restaurant. The memory of one particular evening, when Paul brought Diana here for their anniversary, flitted through her mind, but she refused to give it any attention. She was here to enjoy lunch with her beloved friend and then to tackle her relatively short Christmas list.

Megan was as bright and cheerful as always, and as Diana sat across the table from her, smiling at her friend's extravagant hand gestures, she felt the threat of tears. Quickly blinking them away and dabbing at her eyes with a napkin, she explained that she had something in her eye.

"Oh, you want me to look?" Megan offered. "We can go to the restroom where we can see better, and I'll get it out."

Dear Megan. Of course that's what she'd want to do. Diana swallowed a sigh and smiled. "No, no. It's fine. Whatever it was is gone now."

Megan smiled. "Good. OK, now I've told you what's on my list to find today. What about you?"

Diana began to recount the few items on her own list — mostly just a few presents for Paul and the children. Gifts for their out-of-town relatives had already been purchased and were ready to ship. And, of course, she wanted to get something for the McDonalds and also for Virginia.

Their salads arrived by the time Diana was through telling Megan about her list. As soon as they'd bowed their heads and Megan had offered a quick prayer of thanks, they dug in.

"I'm starved!" Megan grinned as she dumped her entire portion of dressing on her greens then signaled the waiter for more. "I know," she said, holding up her hand and stopping Diana before she could make a comment. "I use way too much dressing on my salad, but next to my husband, you already know that better than anyone else." She stabbed a slice of cucumber. "And I know that's why I never lose weight, even though I always order salads instead of sandwiches.

I remember you telling me more than once that I might just as well order a sandwich because there are just as many calories in the bucket of dressing I use." She took a bite of salad and rolled her eyes, no doubt a silent tribute to the taste.

Diana smiled. "I didn't say a word."

Megan washed her salad down with a sip of water. "But you were thinking it."

They both laughed then went back to eating their salads while they waited for the clam chowder they'd ordered, a specialty of the house. Before the soup came, the waiter dropped off a basket of fresh-baked bread, still warm from the oven, "Enjoy," he said.

Megan and Diana exchanged glances. "I thought they'd forgotten us," Megan said. Then she grabbed a slice from the basket and began to slather soft butter on it. Diana followed suit but with a bit less enthusiasm.

"So," Megan said after savoring and swallowing her first bite, "fill me in on Desert Sands Community. I miss you like crazy here, but I'm so glad you and Paul have your own pastorate now. What's it like? Busy, right?"

Diana chewed her bread slowly, giving herself some time to formulate an answer. Busy? She supposed so, though how much of her business was church-related was hard to say.

She swallowed. "Pretty much, especially since I don't have the preschool there for Lizzie and Micah. I've checked around but just haven't found one that felt right. You know what I mean?"

Megan nodded as she stabbed another piece of dressing-drenched lettuce.

Diana sighed. "Those few hours a couple of days a week were a huge help, but now I'm working with the kids myself. Most of it is arts-and-crafts stuff, but I try to work a teaching in along the way."

Megan nodded. "Oh, you're good at that, and I know the kids love it. But what about the church? Have you met many people there yet? And what part of the ministry are you responsible for?"

Apparently she needed to remind Megan of the size of their church, though she knew she'd told her about it before. "I haven't met a lot of people there yet because there aren't a lot of people to meet. Our congregation has grown a little these past months, but even if every one of them came to one service, I doubt we'd top 60."

Megan shrugged. "What's wrong with that?" She leaned forward. "Personally, I love small churches. Reminds me of the old country church we went to when I was little. Of course, it has its downside too. Obviously a little church can't begin to compete with the larger ones when it comes to children's or music ministries or outreach to the community. But who's competing, right? We can pray and make ourselves available, but only God can bring the increase."

Diana nodded, knowing which Scripture her friend referred to. "Very true," she said. Before she could go on, their bowls of hot clam chowder arrived, and the ladies forgot about talking for a little while.

Diana was pleased with her purchases, though she'd had to push herself to climb back into the car and head home. But it was already dusk, and she knew she needed to get back and rescue Paul. As sweet as it had been for him to offer to take care of the children, she didn't want to take advantage, even though he'd assured her he could cover lunch and dinner.

Diana wasn't hungry at all. After the wonderful lunch she and Megan shared, they'd hit the mall, and even while they focused on looking for Christmas gifts, they managed to squeeze in a stop at the food court for hot pretzels and cheese.

After the two friends parted ways, Diana had disciplined herself not to drive by her former house, though she was tempted. She knew it would only make it more difficult to leave, so she headed straight for the highway.

What part of the ministry are you responsible for? Megan's question, which Diana had deftly avoided answering, still echoed in her ears. True, Diana pitched in whenever and wherever there was a need she could fill, but as far as an actual "part of the ministry," she imagined she'd have to wait until the congregation grew to a more substantial size.

But if the church were already bigger, what areas of ministry would I want to fill? She knew a pastor's wife was usually expected to handle the women's ministry, and she had helped Pastor Mark's wife, Julie, with that at Dayspring. But helping someone else run it and running it yourself were two entirely different things. Though she liked the idea of getting a women's ministry going at some point, she felt she needed more input from people like Virginia first.

Virginia. She'd gotten to know a few ladies from Desert Sands Community, but lately she'd realized how much she enjoyed Virginia's companionship and input, not to mention her expertise in so many areas. Yes, Virginia was indeed the perfect role model for her, and she decided she would make a conscious effort to spend more time with her. *Rather than wait too long like I did with Alice Bosworth. The last time I saw her was to thank her for that soup she made. Meatball soup, I believe it was. Delicious! I told her how much I'd like to have the recipe, but she told me she didn't have it written down.*

Diana smiled as she remembered Alice pointing to her head and saying, "In here. That's the only place I have it. So I guess you'll have to come to my house and help me make it soon, yes?"

Yes. Diana had said she would do that, but she never got around to it. And now it was too late.

Tears threatened to rise up, but she pushed them back down. *No. I'm not going to let that ruin my nearly perfect day. It was absolutely lovely, Lord. Thank You!*

She was almost home now, and she'd just spoken with Paul, who called to ask for an ETA. He said he was only calling because they missed her, but she wondered if they were trying to figure out how quickly they needed to clean up the day's messes before she arrived.

Desert Sands Community came into view then, and as she turned down the driveway and went past the church, she was puzzled to see the house in darkness. *Why doesn't Paul have some lights on? What's going on?* Her heart began to race as she considered the many implications, but she ignored them as she jerked the car to a stop, turned off the engine, and nearly ran toward the door. As she fumbled with the door handle, the door swung open and lights seemed to explode all around her.

"Surprise!"

Variations of the word erupted from all three of them, though the children bounced up and down and squealed from excitement as they continued to shout the word.

Nearly awestruck, Diana stood with her mouth agape, letting the bits and pieces of information about her "surprise" fall into place. The entire front porch was outlined in lights, as was the front door. And when the children each took a hand and led her inside to the front room, she nearly wept at the sight of the decorated tree in front of the picture window.

"Do you like it, Mommy? I helped Daddy with everything."

Diana glanced down at Lizzie's glowing face and finally managed to find her voice. "I love it. It's . . . it's beautiful."

"I helped, too!" Micah pulled on her pant leg, and she turned her attention to her son.

"I can tell," Diana said, smiling now. "It's absolutely wonderful."

She looked at Paul then, who seemed nearly as excited as their children. "So this is what the three of you did all day while I was gone?"

"We did indeed." He took her arms and pulled her in for a kiss. "We wanted to surprise you."

"Well, it worked. I had no idea . . ."

Micah was pulling on her pant leg again. "We made cookies, too," he announced. "Stars and snowmen and — "

"Come on, Mommy," Lizzie insisted, taking her hand. "We even made hot chocolate."

Allowing herself to be pulled into the kitchen, she *oohed* and *aahed* over the not-quite-perfect cookies that greeted her. When tears pricked her eyelids, she didn't worry about blinking them away. While she had been out shopping for her family, they had put together one of the nicest gifts she'd ever received.

Whed Diana opened her front door on Tuesday morning, she was surprised to see Virginia Lopez standing on the porch. She was bundled up against the cold wind that had started up during the night and continued to blow despite the tepid sunshine overhead.

"Virginia! What a nice surprise. Please, come in. I'll make us some hot tea."

Virginia waved away her offer. "No, I can't, mija. Not today. I just wanted to bring this soup over to you. God woke me up in the middle of the night and told me to make this and bring it to you for you and your family." She turned back and pointed to her older model Honda Civic. "But it's in the car, and I'm afraid it's too heavy for me to carry. I was praying this morning and asking God to help me get that soup into the car, and here came my son, Albert. He said he'd been thinking of me and thought he'd stop by and say hello." She returned her attention to Diana. "So you see? Ask and you shall receive."

Diana smiled. She knew that Scripture well, and she too believed that God is faithful to answer our prayers. But somehow she knew Virginia had personally seen that prayer answered countless times throughout the years. She wondered if her own faith would be as strong as Virginia's when she reached her age.

"Sure. I'll get it and bring it in." The moment she stepped out onto the porch a cold blast of wind urged her to walk faster. Within moments, she had retrieved the delicious smelling soup from the floor on the passenger's front side. And she'd just been wondering what to fix for lunch! This was perfect, and her mouth was watering already.

Virginia still stood at the front door as Diana entered the house. "Are you sure you can't come in for a while?" Diana asked. "Maybe just long enough for a quick cup of hot tea? I got some of that White Chocolate Obsession you love. And besides, that'll give me time to empty the soup into a pot of my own. I'll wash yours out so you can take it home."

Indecision danced in Virginia's dark eyes, but then she nodded. "All right, sure. I can come in that long. I have a doctor's appointment in about an hour, so I really can't stay but a few minutes." She grinned and her dark eyes sparkled. "You know how to tempt me, don't you? White Chocolate Obsession tea. Delicious!"

"And I'll get that tea going right away." Diana smiled as she escorted her guest into the kitchen. The children looked up from their projects. "Look who's here," Diana said. "Mrs. Lopez from church. She brought us some nice hot soup for lunch. Doesn't it smell wonderful?"

Lizzie and Micah hopped down from their chairs and ran to greet Virginia. Then they followed their mother to the counter, where she set down the soup and reached into one of the lower cupboards to retrieve a large pot.

"What kind of soup is it?" Lizzie asked, looking from her mother to their guest.

"Albondigas," Virginia answered. She leaned down to speak to the children directly. "Can you say *albondigas*?"

The children tried and Lizzie did a pretty good job. Diana was about to take the lid off the pot of soup to make the transfer to her own pot when she heard Micah say, "What's a . . . a . . . albon..dig?"

Diana smiled at her son's curiosity.

"Albondigas means meatballs," Virginia explained. "I brought you meatball soup."

Diana nearly dropped the pot lid on the floor. Meatball soup? Was it possible it might be anything like the soup her friend Alice had made for her before she died — the soup Diana didn't get the recipe for because she waited too long to go visit her friend?

Having caught the pot lid before it fell, she set it aside and caught her breath as she peered into the pot. Sure enough, it looked very much like the soup Alice made.

She turned to Virginia. "Do . . . you have a recipe for this soup? I would really love to have it."

Virginia appeared surprised. "Why, yes, I do. I'd be happy to write it down for you. But don't you want to wait until you've tried it, to see if you like it?"

Diana smiled as a warm feeling wrapped itself around her in an invisible hug. "Oh, I'll like it," she said. "In fact, I'll probably love it and want to make it myself one day soon."

Her guest seemed slightly embarrassed but pleased at Diana's reaction. She shook her head and chuckled. "God never ceases to amaze me. I knew He wanted me to make this soup and bring it to you, but I had no idea of all the other little details He was weaving together."

Diana nodded. "You're right, my friend. You are so right." She turned a flame on under the already full kettle before turning back to her job of transferring the soup. "I'll have your pot clean and ready for you to take home by the time the kettle whistles."

"Thank you, my dear. Oh, and I meant to get back to you on what you mentioned to me the other day when you called."

Diana lifted her eyebrows and cast a quick glance at Virginia, but before she could ask what she meant, she remembered. Paul's surprise party. Diana had asked if she might want to help plan it, and Virginia had promised to get back to her in a few days.

"I would be honored to help with that," she said. "I'll call you and we can talk about the details when I get home from the doctor."

Diana felt a sigh of relief rising up. She'd been concerned about putting the entire thing together herself, particularly with her husband working so close to the house that he could pop in at any moment. If she could just use Virginia's kitchen as the planning and preparation place for the party, she was certain it would all come together very well.

When Paul came home for lunch that day, he opened the door to a mouth-watering aroma that he couldn't identify. The cold wind hadn't let up much, and he was looking forward to a warm lunch. But what in the world had Diana made that smelled so good?

"I'm in the kitchen," Diana called out, even as Micah and Lizzie ran to greet their father at the door. As he had so many times before, he marveled at their seemingly unending energy.

"We made stuff out of clay today, Daddy," Lizzie announced as the children accompanied him to the kitchen. "Want to see?"

"Want to see mine?" Micah added, tugging at Paul's pant leg.

"I want to see everything you made," Paul assured them, stepping up to kiss Diana on the cheek as she finished setting the table. He sat down in his chair while the children carefully carried their masterpieces to him for inspection. It was somewhat clear that Lizzie had made some sort of decorative plate, but he was at a loss for guessing what Micah had made.

"This is very nice," he said to Lizzie, watching her face light up as she heard his words. "You did an excellent job."

She nodded, her brown ponytail bouncing. "Yep, I did. It's a plate."

"I knew that as soon as I saw it." He smiled. "When it dries, we'll have to find a place to put it."

"How about in the kitchen window?" Lizzie suggested.

Paul glanced at the corner window, which admittedly had just enough room for one more displayed item. It already held a vase of flowers picked by the children and a couple of other questionable art projects. "I think that would be perfect, Lizzie."

"What about mine?" Micah demanded, holding up his project for his father to see. "Where can we put it?"

Paul was relieved that his son hadn't asked him to guess what he'd made, so he gladly answered his other question instead. "How about on the window sill in your bedroom?"

Micah seemed to consider the suggestion for a moment. He nodded. "Yep. Then I can see it every morning when I wake up."

"Absolutely!" Paul darted a look at Diana, who grinned, no doubt knowing he was hoping not to be asked to identify Micah's masterpiece.

"I'm glad you like the bird nest Micah made," she said. "I think it's the nicest clay nest I've ever seen."

That Diana — what a diplomat! "I'd have to agree about that. Definitely the nicest one I've ever seen, too."

His attention went back to Diana. "So I have to ask. What's the masterpiece you've concocted in that pot? The smell is making my stomach growl."

Diana went to the stove, lifted the lid, and smiled. "It's meatball soup — albondigas."

Paul felt his eyes go wide. "You mean, like Alice Boswell used to make? How did you manage to get the recipe?"

"I didn't." She took four bowls from the cupboard and began to ladle the soup into them. "And I didn't make it either. Virginia Lopez made it and brought it over." She stopped what she was doing and looked at Paul. "She said the Lord woke her up during the night and told her to make albondigas soup and bring it to us. How do you like that?"

"I like that just fine. In fact, you can let her know that anytime God tells her to make something special, she's more than welcome to bring it over here." He got up and went to the stove to help Diana carry the steaming bowls to the table.

"I must admit something though," he said as he set a bowl in front of Lizzie and one in front of Micah. "I remember how much you liked the albondigas soup Alice used to make, and I know you felt bad that you never did get over there to get the recipe, so Virginia's timing couldn't have been better. I don't doubt for a minute that God had her bring it to us."

Diana set a bowl of soup down at Paul's place and one at hers. She smiled at her husband, her heart feeling lighter than it had in awhile. "I think you're right."

"Virginia, your albondigas soup was a real hit around here. I can't tell you how much we enjoyed it."

The older woman smiled at Diana as they sat at her kitchen table a couple of days later, the children in their rooms for nap time. "I knew you would—not because I made it but because God told me to make it and bring it to you. For whatever reason or purpose, I'm not sure, but I do know that His plans and purposes are always good."

Diana returned Virginia's smile. "Yes, I believe that, too."

The teakettle began to whistle, and Diana hopped up from the table to turn the burner off before the noise woke the children. *If they're even asleep.*

She carried the kettle to the table and filled up the two mugs, each holding a pumpkin-spice flavored tea bag. The aroma was perfect for this time of year, and Virginia had graciously agreed to try something other than her White Chocolate Obsession.

"This is wonderful, mija," Virginia said as she stirred in a bit of honey. "Thank you again."

Diana rejoined her guest at the table. "No, thank *you*. Not only did you bring us one of the most delicious pots of soup I've ever tasted, but now you're giving me your time to help plan Paul's party." She laid a hand on Virginia's arm. "I didn't know how I was going to pull the party off if I had to do everything here. He usually only comes home for lunch, but I never know that for sure. Every now and then he'll just pop in to pick up something he forgot or to check on me and the kids . . . or whatever. Anyway, it would never have worked. So thank you for letting me use your kitchen to store things and then to put everything together the day of the party."

"My pleasure." Virginia took a tiny sip of tea. "Oh, that is really hot! Guess I'd better let it cool off."

Diana smiled. "That's just the way I was with your soup the other day. It smelled so good, and I was so anxious to taste it that I didn't wait long enough and ended up burning my tongue."

Virginia chuckled. "Isn't that so telling of who we really are? We know God calls us to patience, but practicing patience is tough to do. Which, I imagine, is why we 'practice' it, right?"

"Right," Diana agreed. "I suppose that's why Galatians lists it as a fruit of the Spirit. Apart from His Spirit in us, there's no way we can really be patient, can we?"

"Absolutely not," Virginia agreed. "Even as we grow in the Lord . . ." She paused and offered a sly grin. ". . . and you know that's been many decades for me. Anyway, we still resist God's call to sit and wait on Him and His timing. And then, of course, we live in an instant-gratification society that wants everything *right now*." She shook her head. "I'm so glad Philippians 1:6 promises us that God will complete the good work He's begun in us." She leaned toward Diana. "If it were up to us, it would never happen."

Diana joined her friend in a moment of laughter then asked, "Would you like to try one of the children's Christmas cookies? They're a bit misshapen, but they're pretty good."

Virginia readily agreed, and Diana brought a plate to the table. "Like I said . . ." She lifted up a somewhat lopsided tree-shaped cookie.

"Well, I learned long ago that you can't judge a cookie by its shape." Virginia retrieved one from the plate and took a small bite. "Just as I suspected — delicious."

Diana smiled. Now that she and Virginia were working to pull things together for Paul's surprise party, they talked on the phone almost daily and met in Diana's kitchen when they needed a face-to-face. The plans for the party were coming together nicely, and Diana was certain Paul didn't suspect a thing. Now if she could just get the guest list pinned down . . .

CHAPTER 22

I've got some great news," Paul announced as the family sat down for dinner on Tuesday.

After offering up a quick prayer of thanks for the food, he said, "It's about the McDonalds. I had a call from Doug, and — "

"Oh, the McDonalds!" Lizzie's squeal of obvious delight broke in before Paul could finish. Alternating a pleading look between Diana and Paul, she begged, "Can Sarah come over again? Please?"

"Not today, Lizzie," Diana answered, leveling a firm look at her daughter. "It's too late. But soon. We'll talk about it later. Can you tell Daddy you're sorry for interrupting?"

Lizzie's shoulders sagged as she looked down at the table in front of her. "Sorry, Daddy," she mumbled.

Paul patted the girl's hand. "Apology accepted," he said, then went on with his story. "As I was saying, Doug McDonald called me at the office and told me he's found a job. Well, Albert helped him find it, actually. It seems Albert's longtime friend, John Hardy, owns that insurance company we've seen down on Main Street. You remember the one, right?"

Diana nodded.

"Well, apparently John's been wanting to semi-retire for a while, but he needed to find someone qualified to take over the office. I didn't realize Doug had that kind of training and experience, but Albert knew and got the two of them together. Doug starts work tomorrow, and once he knows the ropes, he can take over for John — meaning John can semi-retire, as he's wanted to do for a while now. He's in his early sixties and wants to keep his hand in the business but not full-time. So this sounds like a perfect solution. Doug is thrilled."

"That's wonderful!" Diana exclaimed, her heart soaring as she thought of how excited and relieved the McDonalds must be. "I'm so happy for them."

Lizzie laid down her soupspoon and raised her hand. Paul and Diana exchanged a questioning glance.

"Yes, Lizzie," Paul said, smiling at his daughter. "What is it?"

"Does that mean Sarah can come over and play?"

"I'm sure it does," Diana answered, "but we'll talk about that later."

Lizzie put her arm up again. Amused, Diana acknowledged her.

"When is later?" the girl asked.

"I don't know," Diana said, "but I'll call Sarah's mother this week and see what we can work out. How's that?"

Sarah's face lit up, and she clapped her hands together. "Oh, goodie! I can't wait!" She turned to Micah. "My friend Sarah is coming over."

Micah looked puzzled, as if he couldn't figure out what was going on that had his sister so excited. He just shrugged and went on eating.

Paul scarcely had time to open the church and get the coffee going that following Friday morning before he heard a knock on his office door. He'd been going through some mail, deciding which pieces to throw away, when he looked up and saw Mitchell standing in the open door.

"Good morning, Pastor," the old man said, his smile lighting up his face and making him appear somewhat younger than Paul knew he was. "Have you got a few minutes?"

Puzzled, Paul glanced at the clock on the wall. It was only a few minutes after nine, and they usually met for prayer on Wednesday. Had he forgotten something?

"Don't worry," Mitchell said, waving away Paul's obvious confusion. "You haven't forgotten anything. I know this isn't our usual prayer day, but I just didn't want to wait that long to come and rejoice with you about all the great things going on here at Desert Sands Community. God has really been at work, hasn't He?"

Paul certainly couldn't deny that, but then he personally believed God was at work in His people all the time, so what exactly did Mitchell have in mind? "You're right, of course," Paul said. "And yes, I have a few minutes. Come on in and sit down. I just got the coffee going."

"Well, I won't turn that down. But I just heard yesterday that Doug McDonald got a job." He sat down in one of the two chairs across from Paul. "Not only am I happy for Doug and his family, but this means John Hardy will finally have more time to go fishing." He leaned forward, his eyes twinkling. "Do you know how long I've been trying to get him to go fishing with me? At least once a week. Isn't God amazing? He knows exactly what He's doing, doesn't He?"

Again, Paul couldn't argue. He absolutely believed that God knew what He was doing, and that His purposes were always fulfilled, regardless of the situation or circumstance. He nodded. "You're right. God is indeed amazing. I love to see how He works all things together for good, according to His Word."

"And that's not all. Now the McDonald family is coming to church regularly, and I know it's just a matter of time — and probably not much time, at that — until Doug and Marie both give their hearts and lives to Christ. After all, it hasn't been long since Byron's son, Max, accepted Jesus as his Savior." He stopped for a moment. "By the way, any updates on Max's situation?"

Paul shook his head. "Not really. I do know Byron isn't going to lose his house. I also know that Max is plugged in with the jail chaplain and reading his Bible daily now. Like Byron told me the other day, whatever happens to Max as far as sentencing, at least we know he's right with the Lord. And God can use us anywhere, amen?"

"Amen!" Mitchell beamed with obvious joy as he listened. Then he said, "Well, then, you can see why I had to come by this morning rather than wait until next Wednesday."

The thought crossed Paul's mind that Mitchell could have called ahead and avoided a possible trip to the church for nothing. But then he reminded himself that the elderly man always said he loved to walk, especially when that walk took him to the church he had loved for so many years and now rejoiced that it was filling up with people once more.

"You are absolutely right," Paul said. "And I'm glad you did."

"Then let's get to it," Mitchell said. "It's time to praise the Lord!"

As Mitchell closed his eyes and began to speak words of thanksgiving and praise to God, Paul did the same, realizing what a wonderful gift God had given him in the person of Mitchell Green. *Is it possible You've given Diana a similar gift through Virginia Lopez?* He shot the silent question heavenward then rejoined Mitchell in expressing his gratitude.

That afternoon while the children were napping, Diana followed through on her promise to talk to Sarah's mother to see about her coming to visit Lizzie. She called Marie, who excitedly declared that "very soon" she'd be able to reciprocate and have Lizzie over.

Before Diana could ask if that meant Lizzie would be visiting them at Albert and Karen's, Marie went on with her good news. "I can't believe how wonderfully things are working out since we ended up here in Desert Sands. When our car broke down here, we were devastated. But then we met Albert, and he offered us a place to stay. And he and Karen have been so nice to us—not to mention that Sarah has inherited a new grandmother. She absolutely adores Virginia! Then you all welcomed us at your church, and now we have so many nice friends here. And since Doug started his job, he's been so happy and full of energy, I can hardly keep up with him."

She laughed, and Diana joined her as they continued to chat about Doug's new job and their family's increasing involvement at the church.

"Oh, and did I tell you the latest piece of wonderful news?" Marie sounded nearly breathless as she asked, so Diana listened intently.

"We're getting our own place! That's why I said we can reciprocate and have Lizzie over to visit soon. It's a two-bedroom apartment, not far from the church. Karen found it for us. She knows the landlord. Anyway, when Doug gets his next paycheck, we'll have enough to move in because the landlord isn't going to make us pay a deposit or anything—just the first month's rent."

"Marie, that's fantastic! Wow, you weren't kidding when you said this was wonderful news." She paused then, as a thought popped into her head. "But what about furniture, dishes, pots and pans . . . ? You didn't keep all the ones you had before, did you?"

"No. We had no place to put them. We kept a few pieces, personal things, but that's about it. But Doug and Karen have a lot of things in their attic that they're going to let us have, and the landlord said the previous tenants left some furniture behind, so I think we're going to be OK, at least for starters."

Diana's eyes watered as she marveled at God's provision. "You know, Marie, I have more sheets and towels than one family can ever use. You're welcome to as many as you need."

As they chatted for the better part of an hour, Diana felt tears pop into her eyes more than once. By the time they finally hung up, she was so full of joy that she wouldn't have been surprised if her heart had soared right out of her body and on into the heavens.

CHAPTER 23

Paul's birthday was less than two weeks away now, and Diana alternated between telling herself everything was under control and would turn out just fine — and despairing that it would never come together.

"It doesn't need to be perfect, mija," Virginia said, patting Diana's hand as they sat at Diana's kitchen table, once again sipping hot tea as they decided on decorations and food. "I say, keep it simple. You can decorate beautifully without going overboard. And as for the food, I really do believe you're right to go with the Mexican food theme. You told me yourself that Paul absolutely loves Mexican food — enchiladas especially — and I just happen to be the best Mexican food cook in town." Her brown eyes twinkled as she smiled.

Diana sighed. "You're right. I know you are. And the menu sounds fantastic — enchiladas, rice and beans, salad, and his favorite German chocolate cake for dessert. How could he *not* love it? But . . ."

"But what, my dear? Are you worried that the cake breaks the Mexican food theme by being German?"

Virginia ended her question with a chuckle, and Diana joined her. "OK, enough, I promise. I just need to stop micromanaging everything. I do that, don't I?"

Virginia raised her eyebrows and shrugged. "Just a bit, maybe."

They laughed again then Diana said, "But here's my concern. There's no way in the world I want you stuck in your kitchen for two days making enchiladas. That's just way too much for you at — "

She caught herself, but Virginia immediately picked up on what she'd been about to say. "At my age. That's what you were thinking, isn't it?"

Diana felt her cheeks flush. "I'm afraid so. Sorry."

"Don't be," Virginia insisted. "It's not the first time someone has alluded to my age, but at least you did it out of concern for me." She patted Diana's hand again. "I'll let you in on a little secret. I do believe that God is renewing my youth like the eagle's, as the Scripture says — and He's doing it by bringing new, young families into my life — yours and also the McDonalds'. I haven't felt this good in years! But don't worry. I've already recruited Karen and Marie to help me with all the preliminaries for the party. By the morning of the big day, all we'll have to do is get those pans of enchiladas into the ovens in the church kitchen. We can get it done a lot faster that way, but are you sure you can keep Paul away from here — the house *and* the church — until it's time for the party?"

"I've got that part under control." She grinned. "The kids are helping, and they don't even know it. We've all three convinced Paul that he should do something special with Micah that day so Lizzie and I can make a nice family dinner to celebrate his birthday. Micah insisted they do the go-cart thing again, but if the weather doesn't cooperate, they're going to the movies. Either way, we'll have several uninterrupted hours to finish all those last-minute details before they get back."

Virginia glanced at the list that lay on the table between them. "So I guess the only thing left is to pin down a final number of guests so we'll know how much food we need."

Diana nodded. "Yes. Well, I think I'm making progress on that front. Our senior pastor from Dayspring, Mark Reeves, and his wife, Julie, are coming, plus our close friends, David and Megan Kellogg. But that's it from Port Mason since the people who initially came to help us get the church started can't make it that day." She shook her head. "I just decided I can't possibly invite everyone from there, so I'm keeping it to those two couples. Other than that, it will be you and your family, the McDonalds, of course, and anyone else from Desert Sands Community that can make it. I've been calling church members, and I don't think I've missed anyone."

Virginia nodded. "Perfect. All right, let's divide up the names of anyone who hasn't yet confirmed, and we'll pin them down so we can get that final count." She smiled. "It's coming together well, mija."

Diana sighed. "I hope you're right, Virginia. But I could never have made this happen without you."

That evening, as the family sat down to a light meal of baked chicken and mixed veggies, Diana noticed that Lizzie seemed to be studying her dad. After a few moments, she raised her hand.

Diana smiled. Since the day she'd cautioned her daughter about interrupting, the girl had made it a practice to raise her hand when she wanted to speak. Even Micah was following suit, and though it was as much from what they'd learned in preschool and in children's church as it was a result of Diana's words of instruction, she was pleased.

"Thank you for being so polite. Daddy and I are very proud. But you don't always have to raise your hand before speaking; you just have to make sure no one else is already speaking. Understand?"

A look of confusion flitted across the girl's face, but then she nodded. "I think so, Mommy. But I want to ask Daddy a question."

Diana lifted her eyebrows and glanced at Paul, who was taking in the conversation with a slight smile. "All right, sure," she said. "You have the floor."

The look of confusion was back on Lizzie's face as she looked down for a moment and then back up. Apparently deciding to dismiss her confusion regarding "having the floor," she said, "Daddy, I heard Mommy say it was almost your birthday. How old will you be?"

Paul grinned. "How old do you think I'll be?"

Diana watched as Lizzie struggled with the answer. Even Micah was paying attention, no doubt wondering if numbers went that high.

At last Lizzie ventured a guess. "Eighty?"

Paul and Diana burst into laughter, though they quickly brought it back under control. Diana knew neither she nor Paul wanted to make their daughter feel as if they were making fun of her answer.

"I'm sorry, Lizzie," Paul said, reaching across the table to lay his hand on her arm. "You gave a good answer, but it's quite a bit higher than my real age. Eighty is closer to Mrs. Lopez's age."

Lizzie's eyes widened, and Micah dropped his fork onto his plate. "Daddy's not *that* old," he declared, turning his attention to his sister, who glared at him in response.

"Actually, I'm going to be 40 on my next birthday," Paul explained. "Forty is half of 80. So I'll have to live 40 more years before I'm 80."

"You're going to be *really* old then!" Micah exclaimed.

Paul smiled at his son. "And when I'm 80, that means you'll be 43 and Lizzie will be 44. And Mommy will be 73."

Lizzie gasped and Micah slapped his hand on his forehead, as if it were just too much to take in. Diana decided to intervene.

"OK, enough talk about ages. Let's finish dinner so we'll have time for stories before bedtime."

"But . . ." Lizzie obviously wasn't ready to let the subject drop. She turned her eyes on Diana and then back to her father. "Can we have a party for your birthday, Daddy? With cake and balloons and presents? I heard Mommy talking to Mrs. Lopez about your birthday. Can Mrs. Lopez come to your birthday party?"

Diana's heart did a stutter-step, as she wondered what else her daughter might have overheard — and how much she was ready to blurt out at any moment. She opened her mouth to try and change the subject, but Paul had already jumped in with his answer.

"Honey, I don't need a big birthday party. Mommy said you're going to help her make my cake and a special dinner, and I'm going to take Micah somewhere that day while you two girls are cooking. Then we'll all have a wonderful family dinner when we get home."

"And cake!" Micah declared, his face shining. "What kind? I want chocolate."

Diana smiled at her son. "Daddy gets to pick what kind because it's his birthday. On your birthday, you can pick."

Micah turned to his father. "Pick chocolate, Daddy. Please!"

Paul looked from one family member to another and then finally answered, "Well, to be honest, German chocolate is my favorite, so if you two ladies want to make me one for my birthday, I'd be happy to help you eat it."

Micah clapped his hands together. "Yay! We're having chocolate cake!"

Lizzie looked at her mother. "Do we know how to make the best chocolate cake ever? Because if we don't, Sarah does, and she can come over and help us."

Deciding the wisest course of action at that point was to agree and move on to another subject before Lizzie revealed whatever else she might have overheard between her mother and Mrs. Lopez, she nodded. "All right, German chocolate it is. And yes, Lizzie. If Sarah wants to come over and help us make the best German chocolate cake ever, she is welcome to do so. Her mom too, if she'd like."

That was a close one, she thought. *I'll have to remember to double-check their bedroom doors before Virginia and I have another planning meeting during nap time.*

It was obvious that Lizzie was ecstatic. Sarah was spending the day with Diana and the children while her parents moved into their new apartment, and the two girls were busy playing with their jump ropes in the front yard.

Diana smiled as she looked out the picture window at the happy, chattering girls. They paid little attention to three-year-old Micah as he rode his tricycle nearby.

Diana wrestled with going back to the kitchen and getting the meatloaf made for dinner that evening . . . or sitting on the front porch watching the children as they played. It was such a nice day, and she finally decided she could make the meatloaf a bit later as easily as doing it now. Grabbing a light sweater to throw over her shoulders, she headed outside.

The girls scarcely noticed she'd joined them. It didn't take Micah long, however, to spot her then leave his trike behind and run toward the porch.

"How come you're sitting outside?" he asked, standing directly in front of her.

She smiled. "Because it looked like a beautiful day out here, so I thought I should come out and enjoy the sunshine with you. Do you think that's a good idea?"

His blue eyes sparkled as he grinned and nodded. "I like it." He looked back toward the yard and pointed. "You want to watch me ride my bike?"

Diana knew that if Lizzie had overheard him, she would quickly have corrected him. "It's a trike, not a bike. Bikes have two wheels, not three." But regardless of how many times his sister pointed this out, Micah continued to call his dark blue tricycle "a bike." Unlike Lizzie, Diana felt no need to correct him.

"Sure," she said. "I'll sit right here and watch you."

Micah raced down the porch steps and out to his trike, where he immediately jumped onto the seat then looked back toward the porch, no doubt to confirm that his mother was indeed watching.

Diana smiled and waved, and he returned the gesture before pushing his pedals and taking off on a trek around the perimeter of the yard. She sighed, thinking again how quickly he'd grown. She already had to be careful not to call him her "baby," as he would quickly point out that he was *not* a baby. As pleased as she was to see both of her children growing up healthy and strong, she had to admit to feeling a bit nostalgic at the thought.

But when she considered how God had blessed her so abundantly, and how grateful the McDonalds were to be moving into a small place of their own, filled with used furniture and other necessities, she shot up a quick prayer. *Forgive me, Lord. I don't mean to be ungrateful. You've given us so much, Father. Thank You!*

It was the last Saturday before Christmas, Paul's fortieth birthday, and he and Micah were headed out to spend the day doing "guy things" while Diana and Lizzie stayed home to prepare a special birthday dinner.

As he neared the freeway exit that would take him and his son to the park where they could rent go-carts, he glanced in the rearview mirror at Micah's glowing face. The boy had absolutely loved their first experience at go-carting, and he'd been thrilled at the prospect of going again. Paul chuckled as he silently admitted he was looking forward to it himself. *I guess there are some things us "boys" don't outgrow—even at 40. But I have to remember that Lizzie said she wants to come next time. Doesn't have to be just the boys all the time. I'm just glad this place has go-carts built so even little ones can ride in them.*

He heard an excited gasp from the backseat, as Micah must have recognized where they were. "We're here! We're here! Look, Daddy, there it is!"

Paul nodded. "You're right, buddy. There it is. I think I'm almost as excited as you are."

Paul parked the car and went around to the back to get Micah out of his car seat. As soon as he unlocked the belt, the excited child all but bolted into Paul's arms. Paul could nearly feel the excitement buzzing through the three-year-old's body as the boy leaned into Paul's shoulders and head.

"This is so cool, Daddy! This is really, *really* cool!"

Paul laughed. "Cool, eh? I don't think I've heard you say that before."

Micah didn't respond. "Look! There's the place where we get the tickets for the go-carts!"

"I see it. How many tickets do you think we should buy? Enough for one ride or two?"

"Enough for a million," the boy nearly hollered. "Or maybe even a hundred!"

Paul was still chuckling when they got up to the ticket window to begin their adventure. The weather was perfect — sunny with an expected high of 70 degrees — and he was out on the town with his best buddy.

Thank You, Lord. I can't imagine a better birthday.

Lizzie had been disappointed when Diana explained that Sarah and her mom wouldn't be able to come and help, but then Diana told her daughter about the surprise party and assured her that the McDonald family would all be there in time for that. At home, Diana was hard at work, alternating between phone calls to and from Virginia, and making sure everything that could be done ahead of Paul's return was indeed done — and done correctly. But it was Virginia who'd become her close confidante these last weeks as they worked and planned and prayed together.

I'm so grateful, Father — as I should be — for how You've blessed me, certainly above anything I deserve and even more than I could ever have hoped or asked for. She shook her head as she used a clean dust cloth to make a final swipe over the furniture in the front room. The tree sat in front of the picture window, lights blinking even at this hour, to signal a pre-Christmas welcome to anyone who dropped by.

"I'll be relieved when Virginia gets here," she mused aloud. "Even though I think it's all under control, I need her sharp eye to do a final check."

"Who are you talking to, Mommy?"

Diana turned to find Lizzie standing in the doorway, dressed in white jeans and a pink shirt — to be changed right before Paul and Micah got home — and staring at her wide-eyed.

Diana smiled. "To myself, I suppose."

"Or to God," Lizzie offered. "That would be better."

Diana laughed, recognizing another great teaching opportunity. "You are so right, Lizzie. It would be better, wouldn't it? In fact, maybe it would be a good idea for us to pray right now and ask God to help us with everything we have to do before the guests arrive for Daddy's party. What do you think?"

Lizzie's nod was exuberant, causing a couple of unruly strands of hair to fall forward. Diana reminded herself to put the girl's hair into a ponytail before the party. Lizzie occasionally asked to wear it down, but Diana didn't think today was a good day for that.

"I think it's a good idea, Mommy," she declared.

They joined hands and voiced a short but heartfelt prayer — Diana first and then Lizzie, who said, "And God, please don't let Micah eat too many pieces of cake and get sick. Amen."

Diana swallowed the laugh that threatened to erupt from her chest. "Thank you, sweetheart. I hadn't thought of that, so we'll have to be careful to keep a close eye on him, won't we?"

Lizzie nodded again, just as the front doorbell rang. "That must be Virginia," Diana announced, heading toward the door with Lizzie right behind her.

"I'm so glad you're here," she said the minute she opened the door and saw her friend standing on the porch, arms full of paper plates and party hats and other miscellaneous items. Diana knew Virginia also had salad and fresh baked *pan dulce* — Mexican sweet breads — in her vehicle. "Here, let me take that. Lizzie, why don't you take Mrs. Lopez to the kitchen while I get the rest of the things out of the car?"

By the time she brought the final items into the house, Virginia had put the kettle on for tea and had even set a place for Lizzie to join them. This would be their final planning meeting for the party, and they didn't want to miss a thing. Then all they had to do was cook the pans of enchiladas, as well as beans and rice, at the church kitchen, where Karen and Marie would meet them in an hour or so. Between Diana's kitchen and the one at the church, they should be able to have it all ready by the time Paul and Micah got home.

Diana's only remaining concern was that perhaps they should have planned to have the party at the church rather than the parsonage. After all, with a confirmed guest list of nearly 40 people, they might be a bit crowded in her modest home.

"Don't be silly, mija," Virginia soothed, patting Diana's hand. "It won't be crowded at all — just cozy. And look how beautifully everything is decorated." She nodded. "Trust me; this is the perfect place for Pastor Paul's birthday celebration."

Paul frowned, puzzled at all the cars in the church parking lot. He didn't remember anything special going on there today, but apparently he'd missed something. Then, as he drove past the church, he felt his eyes widen and his jaw go slack.

"What in the world . . . ?"

There were at least another half-dozen cars parked in various spots between the church and his home. What was going on?

"I think we have company, Daddy," Micah observed. "Maybe they came for birthday cake."

The light came on as he glanced at his son in the rearview mirror. "Micah, I believe you're right." He laughed. "Shall we go join the party?"

Micah fist-pumped the air as he yelled, "Yes," and they quickly exited the car and hurried inside.

Cries of "Surprise!" and "Happy birthday!" greeted them at their first steps into the entryway. Men, women, and children of all ages seemed to spill out of the kitchen and front room, clamoring to welcome the "birthday boy." It didn't take long for Micah to join them.

"I told you, Daddy," he said, speaking loudly over the other voices. "They came for cake!"

Those near enough to hear chuckled at the boy's announcement as they shook Paul's hand, slapped him on the back, and escorted him in to the front room. It had been decorated for Christmas when he left that morning, but now birthday decorations had been added. A large sign, stretched above the mantel, read "Happy Birthday, Pastor Paul." And though no one had told him about the menu yet, he knew it included some sort of Mexican food. His mouth watered at the tantalizing aromas.

There was so much to take in all at once that he didn't notice Lizzie standing at his side. She tugged on his pant leg until he looked down. "Hello, sweetheart," he said, bending down to give her a hug. "Did you help Mommy with all this?"

She nodded, grinning widely. "Yep. Me and Mrs. Lopez and Mommy did it all."

Paul raised his eyebrows. "Is that right? Well, you have all been very busy, haven't you?" He smiled. "And you did a wonderful job."

Then he saw Diana, standing back and taking in the whole scene, smiling as if she'd just pulled off the biggest surprise of her life — which, quite possibly, she had. He held out an arm to her, and she came and joined him. With his family standing near him in front of the fireplace, he thanked everyone for coming. Then, before Diana could retreat to the kitchen, smart phones appeared in the air as people snapped quick photos. When Paul spotted Virginia, he motioned for her to come and join them, thanking her for all her help.

And then Diana and Virginia excused themselves to return to the kitchen. "We'll be ready to eat in just a few minutes," Diana announced before she stepped out of the room.

Paul tried to speak to as many people as he could, marveling that such a large number had fit as well as they did into his front room. He saw Mitchell Green and Byron Phillips, the McDonald family — minus Sarah who, Paul noticed, had joined his daughter near the Christmas tree, where they talked and giggled intermittently. He was overjoyed to see David and Megan Kellogg from Port Mason, and, of course, Pastor Mark Reeves and his wife, Julie, from Dayspring. In addition, nearly all of the Desert Sands Community regulars were there. It was almost overwhelming.

"Time to eat," Diana called as she stood in the doorway. "This is self-serve, and we have extra tables set up in the kitchen and also in the backyard, since the weather has so graciously cooperated today. So come and help yourselves; we have plenty. And we're just so pleased you all could join us."

Before she could go any further, she glanced up at Paul. "Would you like to bless the food before we get started?"

Paul nodded and offered a brief prayer of thanksgiving, followed by another expression of gratitude for all who attended.

When he finished, Diana grinned. "And now, even though we'll repeat this before we cut the cake, can you all help me sing to our birthday boy?"

Micah wrapped his arms around his daddy's leg and joined in singing "Happy Birthday." Then they all began to move toward the kitchen.

CHAPTER 25

W hat a party! You must be exhausted."

Diana nodded, leaning her head on her husband's shoulder as they sat in front of the fireplace, watching the smoldering embers of the fire that had warmed their house and its guests over the past hours.

"I am," she admitted without looking up, "but in a good way. It's almost like I can take a deep breath now, knowing the party went well — and now everyone has gone home and the kids are in bed. We finally have what's left of the evening to ourselves."

Paul kissed the top of Diana's head. "Exactly. And don't get me wrong. I loved the party, and I had a great time earlier with Micah, but this is my favorite part of my birthday. Just you and me . . . together."

Diana sighed, content with the way things had fallen into place. "Virginia was a huge help in putting this together. I don't know how I would have done it without her."

"Oh, I'm sure God would have supplied someone else, but He chose Virginia. And I think she enjoyed it immensely."

Diana sat up and looked into Paul's face. "She did, didn't she? She told me so many times these past few weeks that it made her feel needed. I assured her she was. She also said it made her feel young and strong again." She smiled. "Imagine that. All we have to do to keep feeling young and strong is give ourselves away to bless others."

She moved back to her snug position on her husband's shoulder, and when Paul began to stroke her hair and rub the back of her neck, she closed her eyes to enjoy the feeling.

"So how did it go with Micah today? I'm sure he would have given us all the rundown if you two hadn't been sideswiped by a party when you walked in the door."

Paul chuckled. "I'm sure you're right. On the way home, he said it was his 'bestest day ever.' I asked him about the last time we went go-carting, and he said it was almost as good. I had a hard time tearing him away from there, but I was running out of money."

This time it was Diana who chuckled. "I can imagine. When Micah's having fun, he does *not* want to quit."

"So what about Lizzie? Do you think she enjoyed helping today?"

"Definitely. And Virginia was so good at including her in all our last-minute preparations. Still, I'm glad she didn't find out about the party until after you were gone this morning. She would never have been able to keep such a big secret."

Paul agreed. "That girl likes to talk, and even if she tried to keep that big of a secret, it would pop out anyway."

They sat in silence for a few more minutes then Paul said, "I was amazed at how many people fit into this house — and comfortably too, I might add. I was really pleased to see Pastor Mark and Julie, plus the Kelloggs. But I was even more pleased to see how many people showed up from Desert Sands Community. Must have been close to the entire congregation."

Diana smiled. "Did you notice that Byron Phillips seemed to fade out now and then?" She sighed. "I can't help but think that Max was on his mind. I know he's thrilled that his son has gotten things right with the Lord, but it still has to be tough when he's in a social situation right before the holidays and wishes Max was there, too."

"I can't even imagine how hard that must be. I think waiting for his court date makes it worse. Will the judge be lenient in his sentence or make an example out of Max?" He kissed the top of her head again.

"But like you said, at least we know Max has reconnected with the Lord, and that's really the most important thing for any of us."

Diana nodded. "Did you have much chance to talk with the McDonalds? They must be so excited about Doug's new job and then moving into their own apartment. It really puts things in perspective, doesn't it?"

"Sure does. We are *so* blessed."

"Best of all, they've been attending church regularly — not just Sunday morning but midweek too."

"Want to hear the two very best parts?"

Diana sat up to face Paul. "There's more?"

Paul smiled. "Sure is. Doug took me aside for a few minutes today and told me they were finally able to get the tests Marie needed, but they didn't want to say anything until they knew the results." He paused as his smile widened. "It's not cancer. Marie's going to be OK."

"Oh, Paul!" Diana felt the sting of tears behind her eyelids, but she didn't mind because she knew they were tears of joy. "This is fantastic news!"

Paul nodded. "And here's the second very best part: Doug, Marie, and Sarah have received Jesus as their Savior. They prayed together at home just yesterday, and now they want to be baptized."

Diana could hardly contain her excitement. "Really? Oh, that's wonderful! So when will you do it?"

Paul frowned. "Do what?"

Diana grinned as she shook her head. "Baptize them, of course."

His brown eyes twinkled as he answered. "I'm thinking about tomorrow's service. I first suggested to Doug that we do it the week after Christmas, but he said they didn't want to wait any longer than necessary. So I'll head over to the sanctuary before we go to bed and make sure everything's ready to go."

Diana laughed. "Wow, this is all happening so fast, but Doug's right. There's no reason to wait."

She snuggled up to him, and he pulled her against his chest. Once again she heard his heartbeat and smiled, silently thanking God for orchestrating an even better birthday for Paul than she had ever imagined.

The church was all abuzz on Sunday morning. As Diana and the children sat on the front pew, waiting for Paul to take his place and the worship team to open with singing, she smiled.

The church sounds nearly full, Lord. I know it isn't, but it's at least as full as it's been in many years.

She glanced down at Lizzie on her right then Micah on her left. Both sat silently, though Diana knew they couldn't wait to be excused to children's church after the worship time. What they didn't know is that they would also be staying for the baptism before being excused.

Paul walked toward the podium. He caught Diana's eye before he welcomed the congregation, and the exchanged glance spoke volumes between them. Both were thrilled at what God had done in the McDonalds' lives and also in Desert Sands Community Church in such a short time. Paul had confided to Diana just this morning that he couldn't wait to see what God would do next.

The congregation stood and joined the worship team in singing. Diana was pleased to see that Lizzie tried to sing along when she could. The girl was certainly growing up right before their eyes.

Micah, on the other hand, stood on one foot then the other, antsy to get on with his day. He was *all* boy, that one.

As the singing came to a conclusion, Lizzie and Micah grabbed their Bibles and worksheets, ready to head downstairs before Diana stopped them. "You're staying for one more thing," she whispered. "Then you can go."

Micah sighed and rolled his eyes but didn't say a word, a sizable show of restraint for an energetic three year old. Lizzie just looked puzzled.

Diana spoke just above a whisper. "It's a surprise. Now sit down with me for a minute, and you'll find out."

As they joined the rest of the congregants in settling back onto their pews, Paul took his place behind the podium. His smile took in the entire room.

"We are honored to be part of a very special occasion today," he said. "Some of you already know this, but for the rest of you, let me explain that we have a new family in our midst — the McDonalds, Doug, Marie, and their daughter, Sarah."

Diana snuck a peek at Lizzie, who was now sitting at full attention, her eyes glued to her father.

"As many of us have at times, this precious family recently found themselves struggling financially. As they passed through Desert Sands on their way to look for work in another town, their car broke down."

Paul paused a moment and swept the congregation with his gaze. "We all know that feeling, don't we? When everything that could go wrong does — and then something else even worse happens. Can anyone relate?"

Scattered amens affirmed his point.

"But have you also noticed that the more hopeless the circumstances, the more surely God's presence rises up in the middle of them and makes a way where there seems to be no way?"

More amens quickly followed.

Paul smiled again. "And that's exactly what happened with the McDonald family. They were running out of funds, desperately seeking employment, and then their only means of transportation went out on them leaving them stranded in a town where they knew no one." He leaned into the podium slightly. "But God knew them — each one of them, by name — and He had a plan for their lives. What seemed like the worst possible misfortune on their part was really part of God's plan to establish them in His kingdom.

"Soon after, they met Albert and Karen Lopez, who offered them a place to stay. Then they came to our church's Thanksgiving dinner, where they got to know some of the congregation. Now they're not only attending Desert Sands regularly, but they've all received Jesus as their Savior and didn't want to wait any longer than necessary to openly proclaim their new faith. And that's why today we're having a special baptismal service."

Paul turned toward the back of the stage, where the baptismal pool usually sat covered over. Today, however, it was uncovered, and Paul made his way toward it even as the McDonalds emerged from the wings. All three wore white robes, similar to the one Paul now donned over his own clothes.

Paul stepped down into the water then offered his hand to help each of the others join him. Sarah was the last to step in.

Diana turned to see Lizzie now perched on the edge of the pew, balancing her toes on the floor. Her eyes were wide.

"Welcome, Doug, Marie, and Sarah. We are all so pleased that you've come to join us at Desert Sands, but even more so that you've joined the universal church to which we all belong once we place our faith in Jesus Christ. Is that something each of you has done — received Jesus as your Lord and Savior?"

The three McDonalds nodded, saying, "yes," in one accord.

"And do you wish to follow the example of Christ in baptism, in obedience to His command?"

"Yes," they repeated.

Then one at a time, beginning with Doug then Marie then Sarah, he held them and lowered them into the water. By the time Paul got to Sarah, Lizzie had jumped from the pew to stand on her tiptoes as she watched. Diana was surprised at the level of intensity she saw in the girl's posture.

And then it was over. The worship team was back up front, leading songs as Paul and the McDonalds exited the pool to go dry off and change.

"You can go to children's church now," Diana whispered.

Micah couldn't move fast enough as he grabbed his materials and hurried off after the other children headed for the back of the sanctuary.

Lizzie, however, took her time, her eyes riveted to the baptismal pool as if her friend were still standing there. At last she looked up at Diana and said, "Sarah's only five."

Surprised by the comment, Diana nodded. "Yes, she is." She smiled. "But she's old enough to receive Jesus as her Savior."

After a moment's hesitation, Lizzie nodded, picked up her Bible and papers, and moved off after the other children.

Virginia was exhausted. She'd worked long and hard helping to put together Pastor Paul's birthday surprise, and she'd loved every minute of it. Now, with church over and having witnessed the baptism of the McDonalds, Virginia sat in her favorite spot — in the old rocker that had been her mother's — on the front porch of her home.

"This old rocker and I have seen a lot of good times and bad times together, just rocking and praying and thinking." The old woman smiled. "Sure am glad You saw me through it each time, Lord. You are good and faithful, and I can't imagine what I'd do without You." She chuckled. "Nothing good, that's for sure."

The winter sun was weak that afternoon, but Virginia didn't mind. She was bundled up, as she often was when she sat outside, watching the day pass by. "We do that a lot these days, don't we, Father?" She shook her head. "How much longer are You going to make me wait before You call me home? You know I've been homesick for a long time now."

A soft caress on her cheek told her He did indeed know she was homesick and would come for her soon. "Soon." She sighed. "All right, then. Guess I've still got some praying and waiting to do. But sometimes I wonder what good I am anymore. Can't hardly do anything worthwhile."

A gentle rebuke reminded her that for as long as she remained on the earth, her Father had a purpose for her, as He did for everyone. No one was here by accident, and no one had the right to choose their own time to leave.

Her shoulders drooped and she lowered her head. "I'm sorry, Father. You're right, of course. You have so blessed me to allow me to stay here in my own home, to have my beloved Albert and his family nearby, and to live to see this church reborn in the old building where I spent so many wonderful years as a child and then a young mother."

The thought of all she'd lost during her lifetime — her husband and two of her three children at the top of the list — pierced her heart like a red-hot poker, but she pushed it away. "After all, I haven't really lost them, have I, Lord? I know exactly where they are — with You, waiting for me to join them. So how can I ever feel sorry for myself? You have been so good and faithful to me, Lord — so good and faithful, all these years."

The image of Pastor Paul, standing with his little family as everyone sang "Happy Birthday" to him, brought a smile to Virginia's lips. "Thank You for letting me be a part of that, Lord. I'm so tired I can hardly move, but it was worth every minute of it. And not just because the party turned out so well, but also because you used it to draw Diana and me together." She cast a grin up toward heaven. "You did that on purpose, didn't You? Diana and I each needed a friend, and now, thanks to You, we've found one." She nodded. "I'm really grateful for that, Father—really, really grateful. And yet . . ."

She paused, frowning just a bit. "You know, Lord, no matter how well Diana and I seem to bond and work together, I still feel like there's a little part of her that hurts inside, something she just isn't willing to let anyone see. But You see it, Lord, don't You? And You know exactly what it will take for it to be healed."

Virginia nodded. "All right then. I don't have to know what it is because You already do. All I have to do is pray, so here I am. Give me the words, Father."

And with that she bowed her head and began to petition her faithful Father to once and for all heal the pain in Diana Michaelson's heart.

"Mommy, I know what I want for Christmas," Micah announced the next day as he followed Diana down the hallway toward his room.

Diana stopped then turned around and lifted an eyebrow. "Oh, you do, do you? And just what would that be?"

The little boy's blue eyes sparkled as he gazed up at her. "A puppy!"

Diana felt her eyes widen as her heart did a flip-flop in her chest. "A puppy? Gee, I don't know about that, Micah. That's a pretty big request."

Micah shook his head. "No, it's not, Mommy. Puppies are little!" He held his hands apart from each other just enough to let a bit of sunlight in between. "They're only this big, and they're really fun." He paused. "And I really, really want one. I don't want anything else for Christmas, Mommy. Just a puppy."

Uh-oh. This wasn't the first time Micah had stated his desire for a dog, but now he was making it his one and only Christmas present request.

She smiled. "Well, Daddy and I will have to talk about that. But now it's nap time, so let's talk about this later. Your sister is already in her room, reading, and you need to lie down, too."

"I don't know how to read."

Diana smiled. "I know you don't, sweetheart. But you have picture books. You can look at those or play with your favorite stuffed animals while you rest." She leaned down and touched the tip of his nose. "You might even fall asleep."

Micah shook his head. "Nope. I'm not tired. I just want a puppy."

Diana sighed. "All right. I told you Daddy and I will talk about it. But now it's nap time for you and Lizzie, and I have things I need to do while you're resting."

"You could pray."

Diana blinked. Where had that come from? "Yes . . . I could," she admitted, guarding her words. "But what should I pray about?"

Micah looked at her as if the answer were written in red ink on his face. "The puppy! You could pray that I'll get a puppy for Christmas."

"Micah, Micah . . ." She shook her head, refusing to let herself smile as she spoke. "No more talk about puppies for now." She gently took his hand and walked him the last few feet to his room. Once she had him settled on his bed with three fuzzy friends, she turned to go but was stopped before she could step out into the hallway.

"Don't forget, Mommy. Pray I can get a puppy. Please? And when you talk to Daddy, tell him to pray, too."

Glad her back was to her son so he couldn't see her face, she shook her head and swallowed a chuckle as she walked from the room.

It was midweek, time for Paul and Mitchell's prayertime. Paul found himself looking forward to it even more than he'd expected. He'd had prayer partners before, but there was something about Mitchell Green that especially touched Paul's heart as the man prayed for him and his family. In fact, he'd attributed at least part of Diana's improved attitude toward Desert Sands to Mitchell's intercession for the entire Michaelson family.

The thought still hung in the air as a knock sounded on Paul's office door. He glanced at his watch. *Right on time.*

"Come on in," he called as he rose from his chair to walk around his desk and greet his elderly friend.

Mitchell was using his cane today, something Paul knew he resorted to only when his arthritis flared up.

They embraced and clapped one another on the back before Mitchell lowered himself into one of the two chairs on the visitor side of Paul's desk.

"Arthritis acting up today?" Paul asked.

Mitchell sighed. "Afraid so." He shrugged. "But I'm 82. Can't expect to be in tip-top shape all the time now, can I?"

Paul grinned. "I suppose not, though most of the time you look like you could run circles around me — and most of the others at Desert Sands."

Mitchell chuckled. "Oh, I don't know about that. You look pretty spry, if you ask me." He lifted his cane and pointed it in Paul's direction. "Except for Saturday, when you came home to find a house full of people ready to celebrate your birthday." He winked. "You looked like you could've been knocked over by a feather."

Paul nodded. "You're right. Diana caught me totally off guard. I don't know how she pulled it off, though I know Virginia Lopez played a big part in all that." He lifted a fresh pot of hot java from the coffee maker on the table near the room's only window. "Coffee?"

"Sure. Sounds good. Black, please."

"Got it." He poured two cups, adding sugar and creamer to his, then handed a cup to Mitchell and sat down next to him.

"So . . . anything in particular you'd like to pray about today?" Paul asked. "It seems I usually give you my list and we never get to yours, so I thought we could start out with your requests first."

They sipped their coffee as Mitchell enumerated a handful of concerns, then they put their cups down and began to pray. As they drew to a close and Paul was about to say, "amen," Mitchell laid a hand on his arm.

"Wait," he said. "One more thing, though it's actually about you."

Paul hesitated. "Oh? What is it?"

Mitchell hesitated, and Paul wondered what could be making the man so obviously uncomfortable.

At last Mitchell said, "It's . . . about your wife."

Paul frowned. "Diana? What about her?"

"Well, as you know, I pray for you and your family regularly."

Paul nodded. "And I appreciate it more than I can say."

"I know you do." Mitchell took a deep breath and continued. "Almost from the beginning, when I first started praying for you and your wife and children, something has niggled at me about Diana." He shook his head. "But I could never pinpoint it, so I just left it with the Lord and prayed for her in general. Then, this morning, it came to me — what bothered me about Diana, I mean."

"Go on."

"Pastor, forgive me, please, if I'm out of line, but . . ." They lifted their heads simultaneously and their eyes met. Paul knew the man was speaking from a heart that regularly communed with God.

"You're not out of line, Mitchell. Go ahead . . . please."

The old man nodded. "Did she . . . did she want to move here? Was this something she wanted, too, or was it just you?"

The question hung in the air between them, and despite Paul's efforts to wave it away, it remained there. Yet it made no sense. He knew Diana hadn't exactly been excited to make this move, but it was something they'd prayed about and expected for years. Surely his wife had come around to his way of thinking on it by now . . . hadn't she?

"I . . ." He swallowed, still staring into the depths of Mitchell's rheumy eyes. "I believe she did. Maybe . . . maybe not as much at first, but that . . . was understandable. She had her friends and her routine in Port Mason. The kids were in a wonderful preschool two mornings a week, and I know she hated to give that up. But . . ." He swallowed again. "I'm sure she's . . . adapted by now. She's really come to love this church, the people . . ."

Mitchell nodded. "As I thought. She didn't want to come here, did she?"

Paul felt a defensiveness rising up within him. "It wasn't really that as much as . . . well, as I said, she didn't want to leave the home she loved, the neighborhood, her friends . . ."

Mitchell waited a moment before responding. "As this came into focus for me when I was praying for your family last night, my mind went back to the teaching you gave on Ephesians 5, that well-known section on family relationships. I especially considered how you prefaced that teaching by stressing verse 21 about 'submitting to one another in the fear of God.' You said that as husbands, we needed to keep that focus so we'd always remember to love our wives as Christ loved the church and gave Himself for it — selflessly. True, the Scriptures admonish wives to submit to their own husbands, but that's simply about keeping God's prescribed order in the home. It was the 'submitting to one another' that really impacted me as I thought and prayed last night."

Mitchell paused again, and Paul imagined the man was waiting for him to respond, but for the moment, he was unable to come up with anything to say. But He knew God was saying plenty to him — through the wise old man sitting in his office.

I didn't submit to Diana at all about this move, did I, Father? I didn't ask her if we could pray about it together before I gave my decision to the board. I just decided and told her. Tears pricked his eyes then, and he took a deep breath.

"You hit the proverbial nail on the head," Paul told Mitchell, his voice thick with emotion. "I figured because we'd always talked about having our own pastorate one day that she'd automatically be as excited about this move as I was." He shook his head. "She most certainly wasn't, though she came along without argument and has supported me all the way. But deep down, I knew . . ."

A tear slipped from his eye then, and he felt it trickle down his cheek. "I've been so thoughtless, Mitchell. How could I not have seen it? Or, to be more honest, how could I have ignored it and just pressed ahead with what I wanted, knowing she'd follow me and hoping she'd share my happiness about the move at some point?"

"Don't beat yourself up, my friend. We've all done similar things, especially when our passion is to serve God. We think that because it's a God-thing, then everyone else should see it and fall into line. Sometimes it just doesn't work that way."

Paul nodded, grateful for a friend who was willing to speak the truth in love. Now for a prayertime together before he went home to ask his wife's forgiveness.

Though he'd wanted to go home and apologize to Diana right after Mitchell left, Paul decided to wait until the kids were in bed that evening. He wanted to be sure they wouldn't be interrupted.

After a nice dinner of leftover meatloaf and mashed potatoes, they'd finally gotten Lizzie and Micah tucked in for the night. Now a fire burned low in the fireplace, the tree was lit, and Paul and Diana sat curled up on the sofa, enjoying the quiet.

Paul had prayed off and on all afternoon about how to broach the topic of their move from Port Mason to Desert Sands, but no direct answer had come. All right, so he'd just dive right in and trust God to work things out.

"I owe you an apology," Paul whispered, his chin on top of her head, which rested on his shoulder.

Diana didn't move. "Really? For what? Did you forget to take out the garbage?"

He smiled. "It's a bit bigger than that, I'm afraid. And it's long overdue."

This time he had her full attention, as she pulled back from his shoulder and lifted her head to look him in the eye. "Sounds serious. Should I be worried?"

Paul shook his head. "No. It's nothing to be concerned about. But it is serious, yes."

A burning log popped as Paul shot up one last silent prayer then plunged in.

"I was wrong," he said, taking her hands in his. "When the board told me about this position, I was so thrilled I didn't even stop to consider your feelings in any of it. I just plowed straight ahead on all burners, assuming you'd be as excited as I was." He paused, feeling his shoulders sag. "You weren't. I knew that then, but I was so certain you'd come around. And in many ways you have. But . . ."

He rubbed the top of her hand with his thumb, watching her blue-green eyes for a hint of what she must be thinking. "I was wrong to make that decision without consulting you, without taking your feelings into consideration . . . without praying together first."

Tears pricked the back of his eyelids. "I am so sorry, Diana. I had no right . . ."

Her eyes moved then, back and forth as if studying him in detail. "Of course you had a right," she said at last. "You're my husband, the head of this family. You had every right to make that decision, even if I wasn't crazy about it."

"Technically . . . yes, I suppose I did. But that same passage of Scripture in Ephesians 5 that instructs a wife to respect and obey her husband also instructs the husband to love his wife as Christ loved the church and *gave* Himself for it. Your feelings should have been taken into consideration as we worked through that decision together."

He paused a moment. "Do you remember when I taught on Ephesians 5 recently? I even made a point of including verse 21 about everyone — male or female — submitting to one another in the fear of God." Paul shook his head. "When it came to my decision to take this pastorate and move our family from Port Mason to Desert Sands, I'm afraid I didn't love you selflessly as Christ loves the church. I didn't even consider the need to submit my decision to your feelings and concerns. Something tells me if I had, we would have come to a mutual decision."

Diana squeezed his hand. "You're right. And I'm sure that decision would have been to come here, just like we did. After all, we decided years ago that we'd like to have our own pastorate at some point. We even prayed about it." She shook her head. "I don't know why I resisted it so. I shouldn't have. When I consider all the things that have happened in our family and at Desert Sands Community since we came here, I can't help but believe it was God's perfect plan to move us here."

She reached up to touch his cheek. "I want you to know that I'm happy here now. It just took me a little time to adjust."

"I appreciate that," Paul answered, "but I still owe you an apology for the way I mishandled the entire moving situation. Will you forgive me?"

Her eyes were warm as she answered him. "Of course I forgive you, sweetheart. And even if you did mishandle things a bit, we still ended up where God wanted us to be. Of that I have no doubt."

Feeling a tear slip from his eye and begin to trickle down his cheek, he pulled her close and laid her head against his chest. As he stroked her hair and gazed into the fire, his heart overflowed with thanksgiving to his faithful God.

Diana's emotions seemed to tumble, one over the other, as she rested against her husband's chest, taking in all he had just spoken to her. The more she thought about his apology, the more grateful she became, even as the vague memory she'd been ignoring over the last months reappeared. This time it stuck around until it took on a shape — and she knew exactly what the memory was.

She felt her heart begin to race as she pulled back from her husband and looked up into his eyes. "Paul," she whispered. "Oh, Paul, I . . ."

Paul frowned. "What is it, sweetheart? Are you OK? You look . . . pale. Can I get you something? Some water, or . . . ?"

Diana shook her head. "No," she said, determined to find the words to explain what she had only just begun to understand herself. "No, I'm fine, really. It's just . . ."

She took a deep breath. "It's just that I suddenly understand why I reacted so negatively to your announcement of our move. It wasn't just leaving behind our home and our church and our friends, or even you not consulting me about it — though that was some of it, of course. But . . ."

She paused again, shooting up a silent prayer for the right words. "It's something that happened when I was little — about Lizzie's age. I was crazy about my dad — nearly as much as our daughter is about you." She gulped and dropped her eyes for a moment before lifting them and going on. "As you know, my parents split up about that time, but what you don't know is what followed. And the only reason you don't know it is because I've buried it for so long that I'd nearly forgotten it myself."

Paul lifted a hand to touch Diana's cheek. "I'm listening, sweetheart."

She nodded. "I know. And thank you." Another deep breath. "I scarcely remembered that time — that day, actually — when my mom loaded me into the car, along with a couple of suitcases full of clothes and a few favorite belongings, and drove off I didn't know where, leaving our house behind. When I asked her where we were going, she said it was a surprise. I asked her if Daddy was going to meet us there, and she said no. When I asked her why, she told me we wouldn't be living with Daddy anymore. When I continued to ask questions, she said that was all she could tell me. She said I'd get used to our new home and I'd stop missing Daddy after a while."

Tears trickled down her face now, and she quit trying to hold them back, leaving it to Paul to brush them away. "She was wrong, of course. I didn't stop missing my dad — even when she introduced me to Jack a few months later and said they were getting married and he would be my new dad." She shook her head. "I didn't want a new dad. And even though they kept telling me to call him Daddy, I refused. That's why I call him Jack to this day, though I'll admit he was good to me and did his best to bridge the gap between us."

When she paused again, Paul spoke up. "I can't imagine how painful that must have been for you. But . . . you've told me about your parents splitting up and that your dad died soon after. What I didn't know was how the moving away from your home to a new one came about. And I do know you call your stepfather Jack, but he seems fine with that."

Diana nodded. "I'm sure he is by now. And we have a decent relationship. But . . ."

She struggled to go on, as Paul patiently waited. "The worst part of the story happened a couple of years later, years when I had missed my dad and wondered every day why he didn't come to see me. Mom was married to Jack by then, and one day when I was at the neighbor's house, playing with my friend, I decided to go home for something.

Mom and Jack were in the kitchen, talking, and I guess they didn't realize I'd come home. Something they said caught my attention, and I stopped just outside the kitchen door where they couldn't see me."

Her deep breath was shaky, but she continued on. "They were talking about my dad. Jack said the private detective had discovered that after we left, he started drinking and lost his job . . . and eventually the house." A deep sob racked her body as she pressed herself against Paul's chest. "He said my dad was . . . dead, that he died from the alcohol." She stopped to catch her breath and to pray again before she went on.

Help me, Lord. Please!

Paul stroked her hair and whispered words of comfort until she was able to speak again. She pulled away once more and looked up at the face of the man she knew loved her so very much. "I couldn't accept that when I heard it," she said, "and I guess I've never accepted it, even to this day. I just . . . pushed it away and refused to deal with it. But after I heard what they said, I cried myself to sleep at night, knowing my daddy had died of . . . of a broken heart."

Tears that had brimmed in Paul's eyes now spilled over onto his cheeks. "Oh, Diana, I'm so sorry. I can't imagine how this must have hurt you, especially as a little child."

She nodded. "I guess I just got to the point that I couldn't stand crying anymore, so I told myself Daddy was gone, and now I had my mom and stepdad, and they'd just have to be enough. To be honest, I think that's what helped me come to the Lord soon after that. My neighbor friend invited me to start coming to church with her and her family, and within weeks I'd accepted Jesus as my Savior. His love for me seemed to soothe my broken heart, and somehow I just moved on past that sad time. But now . . ."

She shook her head. "Now God has finally made me remember what happened . . . and how it happened. In my little-girl mind, it was because my mom made me move and leave what I loved most behind. I never saw my dad again, Paul, and I can only hope that somehow he came to the Lord before he died so at least I can know I'll see him again one day." She reached up and wiped away Paul's tears, as he'd been doing for her. "I also realize why I don't feel extremely close to my mom or Jack, but now . . . now I think it's time for me to forgive them so I really can be healed."

She felt a tentative smile touch her lips. "And it all started with a move I didn't want to make. Does that sound silly? Childish, maybe? Do you think it may have had something to do with why I took it so hard when we left Port Mason?"

Paul shook his head. "It doesn't sound silly at all, Diana — or childish. I believe God has used this move to bring your pain from that other move to the surface. He wants to heal your heart at long last, sweetheart."

She nodded. She knew her husband was right. "Will you . . . pray with me about it?"

"Of course." Once again he pulled her close, and as he stroked her hair and she listened to his heartbeat, he prayed for the Great Healer to come and heal Diana's heart.

CHAPTER 27

It was Christmas Eve, and the sanctuary bustled with excitement and joy. Diana was amazed to see how many were in attendance — all the regulars, of course, with several others she didn't recognize.

That's wonderful, she told herself as she escorted her children to the front row. She and Paul had planned a traditional candlelight service, though she knew parents of young children — herself included — worried a bit about lit candles in the hands of their little ones. Still, there was nothing quite as perfect as a candlelight service on Christmas Eve.

The worship team was already warming up, singing Christmas carols to welcome everyone as they entered. Most of the service, in fact, would be the singing of familiar carols so most everyone in the congregation could join in. Paul would give a brief Christmas message, and then everyone would disperse to their own homes for their family celebration.

Except for the ones coming to our house. Diana smiled. Virginia would be there, of course, and Albert and Karen. The McDonalds had said they wouldn't miss it — in fact, Marie had offered to bring lots of homemade Christmas cookies and pumpkin bread to add to Diana's wassail. Mitchell Green said he'd be there "with bells on," and Diana wouldn't be surprised if he meant that literally.

Byron Phillips is coming, too. I'm sure it'll be bittersweet for him, knowing that Max is spending Christmas in jail, waiting for his trial to start in January. But at least he knows his son is right with God now, and that means more to him than where Max will lay his head tonight — or for several nights in the future.

She glanced at her children, Lizzie on one side and Micah on the other, as they sat together on the pew, waiting for the service to begin. She couldn't help but wonder what their reaction would be when they saw the gifts she and Paul had picked out for them.

Lizzie has been begging for a "real bike" with training wheels, so she'll no doubt be thrilled when she sees that bright red bicycle. And Micah? She shook her head. *When Paul brings in that excitable ball of fur tomorrow morning . . .*

How had she let herself get talked into getting Micah the puppy he kept saying he wanted? The boy was only three years old, certainly not old enough to hold up his end of the responsibility to feed and raise the golden lab — not to mention cleaning up after it.

She sighed. Ah well, no doubt she'd end up doing at least part of that feeding and cleaning up, but Paul was right. Children love growing up with a pet, and it was time to bring one into the family, especially since they'd left their goldfish behind in Port Mason.

"There's Daddy," Lizzie whispered, bringing Diana back from her musings. "It's time!"

Diana smiled. The excitement in her daughter's voice was mirrored in her son's shining face. Christmas Eve was such a special, hallowed night, and she was so grateful that she and Paul were teaching their children the true meaning of the holiday and doing everything they could to introduce them to the One whose birthday they celebrated this night.

"Yes, Lizzie," Diana whispered back. "It's time."

The service had ended, most of the congregants had gone home to their own private Christmas Eve celebrations, and the rest had gathered at the parsonage to continue singing carols and to enjoy some seasonal treats. Virginia was the last to arrive, and when Diana opened the door at the sound of the bell, there she stood, cake in hand.

"*Feliz Navidad*, mija," she said, handing over the pan to Diana. "Merry Christmas. Is everyone else already here?"

Diana nodded. "Yes, they're all gathered in the front room, eating and singing an occasional carol. Do you want to come and help me in the kitchen for a few minutes before we join them?"

"Absolutely. I'm beginning to feel almost as much at home in your kitchen as in mine."

Diana set the cake with the red frosting on the counter and took a close look at it for the first time. The green lettering read "Happy Birthday, Jesus." She turned to her friend with a smile. "What a lovely idea!"

The elderly lady grinned with obvious pleasure. "It's something I started doing with my children when they were little. I didn't mind them having the Santa Claus-and-elves-type fun that nearly everyone does, but I wanted to keep the focus where it belonged. So I started baking Jesus a birthday cake every year. We'd gather around it on Christmas Eve and sing 'Happy Birthday' to our Savior."

"Then we'll all do that this evening. And speaking of your children, Albert and his wife are already here."

"I knew they would be. And the McDonalds too, I assume?"

Diana nodded. "Yes. In fact, Sarah and Lizzie are inseparable as usual. And Mitchell Green and Byron Phillips are here too."

"So," Virginia said, "what can I do to help?"

"If you'd like to replenish the wassail pot, that would be great. The ingredients are all right there on the counter next to the stove. I'll get the paper plates and plastic forks for the cake, which I know is going to be a big hit. What kind is it, by the way?"

Virginia smiled. "I didn't dare make chocolate because Sarah insists her mother makes the best chocolate cake *ever*."

Diana laughed. "I know what you mean. I've actually tasted her chocolate cake, and Sarah just may be right."

"I made peppermint cake. I thought it would be something different, and the colors are perfect for Christmas."

As the two ladies went about their last-minute chores and chatted, Diana's heart warmed at the beautiful memories she was already beginning to compile here in her new home in Desert Sands. "Thank You, Lord," she whispered.

"Did you say something, mija?" Virginia asked.

Diana turned to her friend and smiled. "Just thanking the Lord for so very many blessings."

Virginia's brown eyes danced. "So true. We are very blessed, aren't we?"

As Diana nodded her agreement, she picked up the cake and said, "Let's head into the front room, shall we? I can't think of anything better at the moment than singing 'Happy Birthday' to Jesus."

A hush had fallen over the night as Diana lay in bed next to her husband, her head resting on his shoulder. She knew from his slightly irregular breathing that he was still awake, but both seemed content to enjoy the silence.

It had indeed been a Christmas Eve to remember. Only their first one here in their new home in Desert Sands, but she imagined there would be many more. She still missed her friends in Port Mason, but she'd take a drive over to visit them after the first of the year. *Or maybe invite them here instead.* She smiled. Yes. She liked that idea . . . very much.

A timid knock on the door drew her attention, and Paul's too as he said, "Yes? Who is it?"

"It's me," Lizzie's voice announced.

Paul reached over and turned on the bedside lamp. "Come on in, *me*," he said, a smile in his voice.

The door opened slowly, as a pajama-clad four-year-old peered inside, excitement and joy mirrored in her dark eyes.

She's probably too excited to sleep, Diana thought. *Maybe we can let her lie here between us for a while.*

Before Diana could suggest it, Lizzie slipped inside and stood next to Paul's side of the bed.

"You didn't have a bad dream, did you?" Paul asked.

She shook her head. "I didn't go to sleep yet."

"That's what I thought," Diana said. "Too much excitement — and cake."

The child shook her head again. "That's not it. I'm just . . . happy."

"Well, I'm glad to hear that," Paul said. "And does that happiness have something to do with Christmas?"

This time she nodded. "Yep. I really love Christmas."

Paul slid an arm around her waist and lifted her up onto the bed then set her down between them as Diana made room.

"We love Christmas, too," Diana said. "It's a wonderful time, isn't it?"

Another nod. "I love it because it's Jesus' birthday."

"So you liked the special birthday cake Mrs. Lopez brought?"

"Yep. I want some for breakfast tomorrow."

"We'll see about that," Diana said, pulling the covers over her daughter, just as another little voice joined in.

"I want more cake, too."

Paul and Diana chuckled as their sleepy-eyed three-year-old climbed up on the bed and squeezed in between his mother and sister. He was back to sleep by the time his head hit the pillow.

"I was singing 'Happy Birthday' to Jesus in my bed," Lizzie declared. "Then I asked Him what He wanted for His birthday, and He said, 'your heart.'"

Diana lifted her eyebrows and exchanged a glance with her husband. "And what did you say then?" Paul asked.

"I said, 'Here, Jesus, take it.'" She held her arms in the air as if releasing a gift toward the ceiling. "Then I remembered that Sarah told me she asked Jesus to live in her heart before she was baptized, so I asked Him the same thing."

The words seemed to hang in the air as Paul and Diana awaited what came next.

"And He did," Lizzie said, laying her hands across her heart. "I can feel Him — right here."

Hot tears stung the back of Diana's eyes. The child was so young. Could she really understand what it meant to receive Jesus as Savior?

"That's wonderful, Lizzie," Paul said, his voice betraying the tears he restrained. "And what does having Jesus in your heart feel like?"

Lizzie's smile spread across her face. "It feels like . . . home. And it's the best home . . . *ever*."

THE END

VIRGINIA LOPEZ'S ALBONDIGAS SOUP

MEATBALLS:

1 pound ground beef (lean)

2 minced garlic clove sections

½ large minced onion

2 tablespoons flour

¼ cup tomato sauce

½ teaspoon dried oregano

¼ teaspoon ground cumin

1 extra large or 2 small eggs

Salt and pepper to taste

A "dab" of chopped fresh mint

1 small can chopped Ortega green chilis (½ in meatballs, ½ in soup)

Mix together in bowl then shape into meatballs.

SOUP:

1 large pot (holds at least 8 cups water)

½ cup minced onion

2 minced garlic clove sections

1 large chopped tomato

1 chopped jalapeño (optional)

Salt and pepper to taste

1 chopped bell pepper

2 tablespoons chopped fresh mint

Add all ingredients to large pot with 8 cups water, then drop meatballs into boiling water; cook at slow boil for 30 minutes (longer if meatballs are large), then simmer for at least one hour; add salt or other seasonings to taste.

Use the QR reader on your
smartphone to visit us online at
NewHopePublishers.com.

If you've been blessed by this book, we would like to hear your story.
The publisher and author welcome your comments and
suggestions at: newhopereader@wmu.org.

MORE INSPIRING CHRISTMAS STORIES FROM KATHI MACIAS

A Christmas Gift
978-1-59669-416-3
$15.99

Return to Christmas
978-1-59669-442-2
$15.99

The Doctor's Christmas Quilt
978-1-59669-388-3
$14.99

Unexpected Christmas Hero
$12.99
978-1-59669-354-8

A Christmas Journey Home
$12.99
978-1-59669-328-9

For information about these titles, visit NewHopePublishers.com.

THE *FREEDOM* SERIES FROM
KATHI MACIAS

Deliver Me From Evil – BOOK 1
$14.99
978-1-59669-306-7

Special Delivery
– BOOK 2
$14.99
978-1-59669-307-4

The Deliverer – BOOK 3
$14.99
978-1-59669-308-1

For information about these titles, visit NewHopePublishers.com.